Bonnie J. Cardone

Murder Dives the Bahamas

A Cinnamon Greene Adventure Mystery

Also by Bonnie J. Cardone

Fiction
Cinnamon Greene Adventure Mysteries
The Bride Wore Black
Murder Dives the Bahamas
Murder Dives the Caribbean

Short Stories
Murder at the Marietta Inn, *Gone Coastal* anthology
The Last of the Recycled Cycads, *Last Exit to Murder* anthology

Nonfiction
Shipwrecks of Southern California
Fireside Diver

ISBN 978-0-9897165-7-4

Published in the United States of America

Sea Scenes
Santa Maria, CA 93455
http://www.bonniejcardone.com

Dedication

To diving's pioneers and heroes, now fallen asleep:
Hans Hass
Jacques-Yves Cousteau
Lloyd Bridges
Flipper
You inspired generations to dive the deep blue
in search of adventure.

MURDER DIVES THE BAHAMAS

Chapter 1

For two long days we cruised the turquoise waters of the Bahamas looking for Tom Tiburon but in the end, he came to us in a most bizarre way.

The first day of the search dawned bright and sunny. That changed in the afternoon. Dark clouds tumbled in and the once-gentle breeze gathered strength. The air got hot and muggy. Listening to marine radio in the wheelhouse, we learned there was a tropical depression several hundred miles east of us. Captain Mac wasn't happy to hear that.

Long before daylight broke on the next day we knew conditions had worsened, we could feel it in the way the 98-foot *Dolphin Diver II* shifted on the lumpy seas. Tossed around in our bunk and unable to sleep, Danny and I were up early.

"We're shit out of luck," Capt. Mac told us as we went into the wheelhouse to find out what was going on. "That tropical depression has become a tropical storm, likely to become a hurricane. We're heading back to Miami now."

"We haven't found Tom," Danny objected. "You said we could make one more dive."

"I can't risk my boat and the lives of my passengers and crew for one person," Mac said. He looked tired. His thick black hair and bushy mustache were more disheveled than usual. He hadn't shaved recently and stubble darkened his cheeks and chin.

Mac started the *Dolphin Diver II*'s engines and barked an order to raise the anchor. A few minutes later, the boat was underway, rocking and rolling. I braced myself by wedging my body between Mac's chair and the instrument panel.

We'd just begun moving when Mac muttered, "No, no, no, no. Oh no." He picked up the binoculars and stared intently through the rain-spattered windshield, then shook his head as if to clear it. "I'm too old for this," he said, half to himself.

"What?" I asked.

"Take a look." Mac handed me the binoculars.

At first, all I saw were nasty looking swells. Then, at the top of one I saw two sleek gray dolphins, side by side. They held something between them. My heart dropped to my toes. The dolphins disappeared down a big swell and reappeared on another.

"Can't be," I said.

"What is it?" Danny asked. He pulled himself up from the deck, where he'd been sitting with his back against a bulkhead.

The dolphins went down a wave and then, seconds later, were poised on the peak of another. They had a body — a man's body — between them. I thought I knew whose it was.

"It's still there, isn't it?" Mac asked, his voice filled with dread.

"Yes," I said. "It's got to be Tom." I shivered.

"Tom?" This came from Danny, who reached for the binoculars and peered through them before saying, "Holy shit. They're bringing Tom to us."

Mac put the engines in neutral and asked his second skipper to take the wheel. Then he, Danny and I made our way out onto the bouncing deck. As we stood in the rain, clinging to the rail of the pitching boat, the dolphins arced through the water toward us, the body between them.

Tom's short dark hair and bright red swim trunks contrasted vividly with his pale, pale skin. The animals managed, somehow, to keep Tom's face above water while his feet, clad in black wetsuit boots, bobbed in the water near their flukes.

"He can't be alive," Capt. Mac said, echoing my thoughts.

When the dolphins got within a few yards of the boat, they stopped, beaks pointed in our direction. One of them made a chattering sound.

"Damn. I don't think they're coming any closer," Mac said.

Danny didn't hesitate. "We'll go get him."

"I don't think that's a good idea. It's real ugly out there," Mac warned.

"We can't leave Tom here. You coming, Cinnamon?" Danny's blue eyes sought mine.

The waves were humongous. I didn't want to go.

Mac groaned. "Oh no. Not Half-pint," he said, using his

nickname for me. "You'd be better off with the divemaster, Danny. If he wants to go, that is."

"What's wrong with me?" I demanded.

"Whoa," Mac said, raising his hands. "Don't take that wrong. I just don't want anyone else getting hurt."

"I've been diving for 20 years," I said. "I can handle it." My words had a conviction I didn't feel.

As Danny and I grabbed masks, snorkels, fins and divers' versions of life vests, called BCDs, Mac followed us, wringing his hands.

"You're gonna get creamed," he said.

We ignored him.

"You're on your own out there," Mac went on. "Isn't anybody gonna come rescue you."

I knew that but didn't like hearing it said out loud. Neither Danny nor I responded. We put on our BCDs and inflated them by blowing into the hose on the left shoulder.

When he realized we were going no matter what, the captain's practical side kicked in and he came up with a plan, about which we had a brief discussion.

Five minutes later, Danny and I stood at the gate on the port side of the boat looking down at the angry waters. I would rather have been almost anywhere else. Danny's face registered a lack of enthusiasm as well. Holding hands, we jumped off the boat.

Dad must have come out on the deck just then because in mid air I heard him shout, "Cinnamon, no!"

Too late. The water was a welcome relief to the muggy air and felt good on my skin. But the waves, big when seen from the deck of the boat, looked mountainous now. When we were in a trough between them, all we could see were walls of water.

"Shit," Danny said and an icicle of fear knifed though me.

"We've got to go back," I said.

The dolphins were in front of us before I finished speaking. They weren't the spotted dolphins that were the focus of our trip. They were a pair of unusually friendly bottlenoses we'd encountered just once before. Mac thought they might be escapees from a trained dolphin program. We'd named the one with a notch on its dorsal fin Notchy. Scratches on the beak of the other dictated its name.

Up close the body was chalky white. Tom was dead indeed.

"Grab his arm," Danny said, so I did, albeit reluctantly. Tom's skin was cool and clammy. Danny took the other arm. Relieved of its burden, the dolphin nearest me chattered, moved its beak up and down rapidly and looked at me expectantly.

I don't know why, but "Thank you," popped out of my mouth. The dolphin nodded, emitted a high-pitched squeak and dived beneath the water. The other dolphin followed.

Mac had given us one of the boat's lifejackets, now Danny and I struggled with the difficult and distasteful job of putting it on Tom. The body was slippery. Touching it was unpleasant. After what seemed like an eternity the deed was done.

Now we had another problem. The swells were so high we couldn't see the boat. We twisted this way and that without getting a glimpse of it. I found the whistle on my BCD and blew it with as much force as I could. Just before panic set in we heard another whistle. Briefly atop the crest of a wave, we saw Capt. Mac standing on the deck only yards away. He continued to blow his whistle every few seconds, leading us back to the boat. We towed Tom between us.

It was a short but slow trip. Wave after wave broke over us, filling our snorkels; if we didn't constantly clear them with a puff of air we inhaled salt water, which caused choking and coughing. Rain on our facemasks made it nearly impossible to see. The swells tried to wrest the body from our grip.

The whistle got louder. Now the boat was right in front of us, bouncing about on the waves like a toy. My fear nearly overwhelmed me; I didn't think we'd be able to get onboard.

Capt. Mac came to the rescue again. He threw us a line and we clipped it to Tom's lifejacket. Danny and I let go of the body and clung to each other.

"The seas will get calmer," Danny said in my ear. "We'll wait. When I say 'go,' swim like hell."

We floated up and down for what seemed a long, long time. The water chilled me to the bone. I thought we were going die. Then, as Danny predicted, the waves did diminish. Not a lot, but enough.

"Go!" Danny said. I put my head down and kicked with all of my strength. When I got to the dive platform, hands reached down and plucked me from the sea. I scrambled up the ladder to the deck where, trembling and giddy with relief, I grabbed the rail and looked down. Danny was on the dive platform; he, Dad and the divemaster were reeling Tom aboard. They slipped a rope around the body and

—
5

hauled it onto the deck.

Hanging onto the rail, I stared at Tom. His eyes were open and fixed on the sky. The rain beat down upon him.

Even Capt. Mac was shocked into immobility. Time stood still. Then my training as a part-time forensic photographer kicked in. I slid my photo case out from under the camera table and took out a tiny point and shoot. This wasn't the camera I usually used but it was perfect for the current task because it was waterproof. Bracing myself against the camera table, I snapped photos of the body.

"Cinnamon," Danny hissed. "Have you lost your mind?"

That was followed by a hair-raising scream.

"Oh my God, Tom?" All eyes turned to Kimberly, hanging onto the handle of the galley door. Her pale blue eyes, focused on her husband's body, were huge in a face that held no other trace of color.

"What are you doing?" she screeched, lurching across the deck toward me.

Mac grabbed me and pulled me away from Tom. When Kimberly reached us, she clung to Mac, wispy strands of hair whipping across her face. She looked at the body and screamed again.

"Take her inside," Mac ordered, prying Kimberly's fingers off his arm and pushing her toward me. We stumbled toward the galley together. As we went inside, I heard Mac say, "Wrap him in plastic bags and put him in the freezer. Hurry, we've got to get moving."

I led Kimberly to the far end of the galley and made her sit in a booth with her back to the outside door. I didn't want her to see her husband's body being brought inside.

I needn't have worried. Focused on her own misery, she collapsed in a sodden heap, sobbing. I grabbed some towels, draping one over her head and a couple more around her shoulders.

Captain Mac strode through the galley and into the wheelhouse. "Let's get the hell out of here," I heard him say. He put the engines in gear and the boat lurched ahead in the formidable seas.

Chapter 2

Side by side in the wheelhouse, feet braced firmly on the deck and backs against a bulkhead, Danny and I tried to stay in one place on the rocking boat. There was no conversation. That was impossible in the current conditions. The roar of the wind, the heavy rain and the waves crashing down upon our little vessel were deafening, punctuated by the sounds of yet another object coming loose and being hurled about.

Many of the passengers were seasick, something I wanted desperately to avoid. So I focused on better days, reliving our trip, detail by detail. I began with our first night aboard the *Dolphin Diver II*, remembering how shared activities had changed strangers into friends.

We were exhilarated. We'd spent the day jumping into the warm, shallow waters of the Bahamas Banks and snorkeling with spotted dolphins. It had happened not once but several times, which was a dream come true for most of us.

Now, as we waited for dinner, the galley was full of happy chatter. The *DD II*'s seating arrangements consisted of three, four person booths; on this occasion, Danny and I shared ours with two of his former students, Mike Keating and Dave Pecot. Danny had certified them when he was working for a Ventura, California, dive shop, several years before he opened his own store in Cliffview, where we both live.

In their early 40s, Mike and Dave were tall and athletic. Mike had thick dark brown hair, stylishly cut, and intense brown eyes. Dave covered his sparse blond hair with a variety of hats, today it was a UCLA baseball cap, and his blue eyes were nearly always inscrutable behind sunglasses. Both men were married but since their wives weren't divers they took yearly vacation trips together.

I liked the guys instantly. They engaged in a great deal of good-natured and sometimes hilarious ribbing.

Danny and I had just gotten settled in the red vinyl booth when the second skipper stuck his head out of the wheelhouse.

"You have a call, Danny," he said. "Someone named Sam."

"That would be my kid," Danny said smiling. He slipped out of the booth and went off to talk on marine radio.

"I've got kids, too," Mike said. "And I just happened to have a couple hundred photos of them. Because we're friends, I'll show you a few."

He pulled a small photo wallet from the pocket of his shorts and thumbed through it, retrieving three photos, which he pushed across the table to me.

"This is my beautiful wife, Burgie, and my two incredibly intelligent and talented sons," he said. "I took these excellent pictures myself."

The snapshots were of such poor quality it was hard to tell what the three people in them actually looked like.

"My, my," I said, taking the diplomatic route, "your family is very photogenic."

"And incredibly intelligent," Mike reminded me, "not to mention talented."

Dave picked up the pictures. "These are terrible, Mike," he said, delight in his voice. "All of them are out of focus."

"My camera is very sophisticated," Mike complained. "It'll be awhile before I master its many controls and features."

"It's a point and shoot," Dave said. "All you have to do is press a button. I'm surprised Burgie lets you use it."

"Burgie," I said. "How unusual. Is that her real name?"

"Her parents call her Barbara. Burgie is short for burglar. She's really good at picking locks," Dave explained.

"Yes indeedy," Mike said. "It's a skill honed by many years of locking herself out of home and office."

"How long have you and Dave known each other?" I asked.

"Since we were five," Mike said. "The two of us and the Lovely Laura lived on the same street. She was my girl friend until he stole her from me."

"She thought he was pretty cool when she was seven," Dave said. "Luckily, she got smarter as she grew older." He opened his

—
8

logbook and pulled out a photo. "This is the Lovely Laura," he said. The pretty blond in the studio photo looked familiar but I couldn't remember where I'd seen her before.

"'Pretty is as pretty does,'" Mike smirked. "Can she disarm a burglar alarm as fast as my wife?"

"What lucky men you are," I said. "Beautiful wives and really nice logbooks. Especially yours, Dave."

The book in question had a bright red cover with a diagonal white stripe, the classic design of the divers down flag. "David I. Pecot" was stamped in gold across the bottom.

In the past, divers used logbooks to keep track of dive details such as depth, bottom time and surface intervals, needed to calculate how long they could stay at various depths on subsequent dives without getting the bends. Since dive computers do all those tasks for you and also allow you to download the info they collect to your PC, fewer divers keep paper logbooks today.

Dave was the exception. "Mike gave this wonderful book to me," he said. "It's waterproof and has a matching pen," He held up the pen, also red with a white stripe, before slipping it back into a sleeve on the inside cover.

"Dave's into sea creature watching," Mike explained. "He notes what he sees in his logbook. He's even got a life list, like a birdwatcher."

"One hundred twenty-two species and counting," Dave said happily. "I saw my first school of Caribbean reef squid today."

"A truly life-altering experience," Mike intoned, raising an eyebrow.

"What do you do for a living?" I asked Dave.

"I'm an accountant," he answered. "I work for a church."

"Ah," I said, enlightenment dawning.

"'Ah' indeed," Mike said. "This is definitely an accountant's logbook. Everything he sees goes into it. It's all there in itsy-bitsy, teeny-weenie handwriting you need a magnifying glass to read."

"Yet when you want to impress sweet young things with your fantastic knowledge of the underwater world, who do you ask about what you've seen?" Dave looked smug.

"You, of course," Mike answered. To me he said, "He does know his critters. Spends hours pouring through sea life ID books.

"I have to admit, I've found his log useful at times," Mike continued, "especially when I can't sleep. Just one page and I'm out like that." He emphasized his statement by snapping his fingers.

Dave opened his mouth to defend himself but Mike changed the subject. "Did I show you what Dave gave me? Have a look at this." He retrieved a Swiss army knife from a pocket in his shorts and pulled out several of its tools, including a pair of miniature scissors, a tiny saw and a knife blade.

"I gave that to him because I knew Burgie would need it some day," Dave said, "Mike's so mechanically challenged he can't change a light bulb by himself."

"Can too," Mike said.

"Tell her which of the tools you've actually used, Mike," Dave demanded.

"The corkscrew, can opener and cap lifter have figured prominently in my lawyerly career," Mike said.

Danny returned to our booth just then and the cook announced dinner was served. The meals on the boat were fantastic. That night we had filet mignon, baked potatoes, a spinach salad, fresh fruit, green beans and freshly baked rolls. The dessert, the cook's special bread pudding, brought raves from the passengers.

The day's activities and the sea air had made me ravenous. When I finished eating I asked Danny, "How's Sam?"

"He's fine," Danny said. He looked uncharacteristically glum.

"My ex-wife is expecting twins in a couple of months," Danny told Mike and Dave, "Sam can hardly wait for the babies to come, that's all he talks about."

"Twins, wow," Mike said. "How old is Sam?"

"Eight."

"And these are his first siblings?"

"Right," Danny said.

"Well no wonder he's so excited."

Danny's face didn't brighten.

"I'm going to have my first sibling soon, too," I said. "Sandy doesn't have much of a baby bump although she's five months pregnant. Since pregnant women aren't supposed to dive, she'll only be snorkeling on this trip."

"She can't be much older than you," Mike said. "Isn't it weird to have a stepmother the same age you are?"

"She's actually a couple of months younger than me. And it was very weird at first," I said. "Now, however, I'm looking forward to having a brother or sister. It'll be fun, I think."

As we chatted, the boat was cruising to the next site, where we'd make a night dive. The Sugar Wreck is the remains of an island freighter that sank in the early 1900s. We'd heard it was an outstanding site.

When the dive was announced earlier in the day, everyone except our two snorkelers, Sandy and Cathy, had enthusiastically said they'd be going.

Once we got to the site, Jessica and Kimberly pleaded fatigue and opted to skip the dive.

The rest of us waited for dark, then got ready. Just before Danny and I jumped into the water, Kimberly and Tom Tiburon came out on the deck. When they signed up for the trip, Danny and I were excited. Tom was a famous underwater photographer and we were eager to get to know him.

He turned out to be a pain in the butt. Arrogant and demanding, he was continually challenging the crew and other passengers. And now, because he was getting into the water late, he'd be late getting back. The divemaster would have to wait up for him. Since the crew arose at the crack of dawn, Tom's actions were, at the very least, inconsiderate.

I forgot about Tom as soon as I hit the water. I've loved night diving from my very first one, when I was a teenager. Visibility is limited and not knowing what might be just outside your range of vision adds an aura of mystery and excitement missing in day dives.

Twenty feet deep, the Sugar Wreck is the only structure on the ocean bottom for miles and a busy haven for a collection of marine life. The wreckage is scattered over a wide area and none of it rises more than five feet above the seafloor. It is mostly a jumble of metal and collapsed decks, along with two large anchors.

We'd dived here during the day and found fish everywhere. A barracuda or two hung around near the surface, schools of grunts drifted in unison across the bottom and solitary fish peeked from hiding places in the wreckage. I could hardly wait to see what animals used the wreck as a motel at night.

The area right under the *DD II* was in shadow but big bright lights on its deck illuminated a circle around it that stretched several yards beyond the hull.

As Danny and I descended, a small southern stingray glided by just a few feet above the sandy bottom. Danny swam after it, trying to get in front of it and herd it back toward me. I took three photos before the ray flew off into the inky darkness.

The throb of the boat's generator faded as we wandered away from the boat, searching the wreckage. Fish were tucked away inside it, sometimes alone and sometimes in schools. I photographed a French angelfish, a dinner plate sized beauty with a blue face and black body flecked with gold.

Our best find was a male loggerhead at least five feet long. He was asleep on the bottom, using a piece of twisted metal as a pillow. Though the turtle had his eyes closed and was motionless, two large remoras darted around on his back and tried to attach themselves to his eyes. Annoyed, the turtle awakened and craned his head back over his shell, snapping at the hitchhikers. A few minutes later, he rose from the seafloor and twirled around in midwater, trying to get rid of the pests.

When the turtle disappeared in the dark, we moved on. Other than the occasional flashes of other photographers' strobes and the beams of other divers' lights in the distance, we were alone in a silence broken only by our exhalations. I relished the bathtub warm water and tranquility.

We came across a small turtle sleeping on the sand and a spotted moray eel out hunting for dinner before my strobe battery died. I switched to a small backup light and we explored a few more minutes before making our way back to the *DD II*. As we climbed aboard the boat, the divemaster noted the time next to our names in his log.

"How was it?" he asked.

"Super," Danny said. "We saw a huge loggerhead with two remoras."

"Dave was excited about that," the divemaster said. "He couldn't get over how big it was."

"More fodder for his logbook," I said.

We stowed our gear and were on our way to our stateroom when Capt. Mac wandered out on the deck. "Everybody back?" he asked.

"Tom's still in the water," the divemaster replied.

"It figures," the captain said. "What time did the sonofabitch go in?"

"Forty-five minutes after everyone else," the divemaster told him.

"Sonofabitch," the captain swore. "You go to bed. I'll log him in." The tone of his voice left no doubt that Tom was about to get a piece of Mac's mind. I was glad it wasn't me.

In our stateroom, Danny and I showered together — not easy in the tiny stall. Good thing we've had lots of practice at home.

I'd been in such a hurry to get into the water during our first few dolphin encounters that I hadn't put on my nylon/Lycra dive suit. As a result, my back, legs and arms had gotten sunburned. After we dried off, Danny gently applied a soothing, menthol scented cream to my reddened skin. Even that, however, could not keep me awake. I was asleep before he finished.

Chapter 3

We'd been slogging through sloppy seas, Miami bound, for more than an hour. Although many of the passengers and crew were seasick, Danny and Mac were hungry. Danny made his way into the galley and returned with a bag of apples, some cheese and a loaf of French bread. When I saw the food, I realized I, too, was famished.

Eating was a challenge. Mac let his second skipper take the helm for a few minutes and reached for an apple, which slipped out of his grasp and began bouncing about on the deck. Watching it made me dizzy. I tore off a piece of bread and a chunk of cheese, then braced myself on the deck next to Danny and forced myself to recall the second day of our trip.

Danny was up at sunrise, as usual. Shortly after we met he nicknamed me "Sunshine." It's a joke. I hate getting up early, it makes me grouchy. But here, where there were dives to be made and dolphins to be seen, I was up early and downright cheerful about it.

In the galley, I filled my mug with hot coffee and headed for the sundeck, passing Tom, who was working on his cameras. He didn't look up.

Mike, Dave, Danny and Dad were already on the sundeck. Pete and Jessica showed up a little later, followed by Paul. Cathy and Sandy were the last to arrive.

As the sun rose in the sky, the engines were started and we got a brief whiff of diesel fumes before the boat got underway, cruising easily over calm seas.

Sunshine lifts my spirits and makes me happy; being on the ocean fills me with joy. Here, floating on clear turquoise seas with a bright blue sky overhead and those I love nearby, I was nearly delirious with delight.

Breakfast was served as we traveled to the first dive site. The galley always offered a selection of juices, fresh fruit, cereal and eggs cooked to order as well as a daily special. That was thick slabs of French toast the first day and wonderful blueberry pancakes the second.

Jessica and Pete got stuck in the booth with the Tiburons. All four ate quickly and left right away. Danny and I lingered, chatting with Paul and Cathy. Paul, the publisher of the Cliffview Chronicle, has been Dad's best friend for several decades. Cathy, Paul's long-time girlfriend, is his paper's society editor.

My mother, Julie, began touring with a rock band when I was four. She died when I was eight. Even before she left, Dad was my primary caregiver.

Over the years, he and I have spent a lot of time with Paul and Cathy; they're like family. The two of them are as comfortable together as a pair of old shoes. They've been dating forever but live apart and seem in no hurry to change the status quo.

As befits a "society" columnist, Cathy loves gossip. This morning she was dying to tell us what she'd heard the previous night. After making sure we were the only ones left in the galley, she spilled the beans.

"I got up to get a soda last night about 10:30…"

"Soda? She was looking for leftover pudding," Paul said, chuckling and stroking his beard.

"You were hoping I'd find some, too," Cathy said. "Anyway, I had my head in the fridge when the door to the deck opened and Kimberly tore through like a bat out of hell. I heard loud voices outside. The captain and Tom were really going at it."

"We figured that was coming," Danny said, "Tom wasn't back from the night dive when we went to bed."

Cathy continued her tale. "I went out on deck. Capt. Mac had a hold of Tom's arm and was calling him an 'inconsiderate asshole.' He said from now on Tom will dive with everyone else or he won't dive at all.

"Tom said he'd paid good money for this trip and he'd dive when he damn well pleased.

"Capt. Mac said it was his boat and he made the rules.

"Tom said, and I quote, 'No incompetent alcoholic is going to tell me what to do.'"

"Them's fightin' words," Paul interjected.

"You better believe it," Cathy went on. "The captain was furious. He put his hands around Tom's neck. I think he would have killed him except Kimberly arrived with reinforcements. She'd gotten the crew out of bed. The divemaster and second skipper restrained the captain, the deckhand and cook grabbed Tom."

"Wow," Danny said. "It's not very smart of Tom to piss off the captain. I think Mac likes a couple of beers at the end of the day but that doesn't make him a drunk."

Tom and Kimberly walked into the galley just then. Mike had nicknamed Kimberly "The Mouse," and she looked especially mouse-like right now. She carried one of her husband's cameras. Tom was frowning, a near-permanent condition it seemed, and carrying a laptop. He set it down on the table of the booth farthest from us and plugged the cord into an electrical outlet. Next he took the camera from Kimberly and began transferring pictures from it to the computer. It reminded me I needed to do the same sometime soon.

There was silence for a few minutes. Then Tom uttered an expletive followed by, "None of these images is worth a damn. Another whole day wasted. Modeling isn't that hard. How can you be so clumsy?"

"I'm doing my best, Tom," The Mouse whimpered.

"Well your best is unbelievably bad." Tom closed the laptop and jerked the plug out of the wall. He picked up the camera and the computer and strode past us, disappearing down the stairs. Kimberly stood up and followed him. As she went by, I reached out and touched her arm.

"Maybe I can help, Kimberly. Why don't you make the next dive with me?"

She looked at me. Tears ran down her cheek. "I try so hard," she said, "and he still hates everything I do."

Horrified by feminine tears, Danny and Paul beat a hasty retreat, leaving Cathy and me to deal with The Mouse. She sank down beside Cathy, who put an arm around her. Kimberly collapsed upon her ample bosom, weeping.

"There, there," Cathy said.

Kimberly cried harder.

Cathy rolled her eyes.

I searched for something, anything, to distract Kimberly, settling on the silk scarf around her neck. It was beige, with a seashell motif.

"You're wearing a beautiful scarf," I said. "You seem to have quite a lot of them."

"Tom says the scar from my tracheotomy is ugly," Kimberly, said, blowing her nose on the tissue Cathy handed her. "I cover it up with a scarf."

"You had a tracheotomy? What happened?" I asked.

"I caught pneumonia and nearly died," Kimberly explained. She recounted her illness in great detail. By the time she finished, the histrionics were over.

"Has Tom told you what he doesn't like about your modeling?" I asked.

"No, he just says I'm awful."

"Dive with me this morning," I said. "I'll take some pictures and we can critique them afterward. Maybe I can give you some pointers."

Kimberly agreed and all of us began getting ready for the dive.

We arrived at the site soon after. When I told Danny I was going to dive with Kimberly, he looked relieved and immediately teamed up with Dad and Paul. While he enjoys finding little critters for me to shoot, modeling is not his favorite underwater activity and that's what I had wanted him to do on this dive.

Before entering the water, Kimberly and I went over a few hand signals and did a buddy check, making sure we knew how to release each other's weights and could locate the other's octopus regulator. I was pleased at how attentive she was.

The site was El Dorado, a large, relatively low profile reef surrounded by sand. Our first photo subject was a five-foot long nurse shark we found lying on the sand at 50 feet. These are sedentary creatures, not dangerous to divers unless harassed.

I motioned to Kimberly to get close. I thought she might be afraid of the animal but she moved slowly and surely across the sand until she was only two or three feet from it.

The shark proved skittish. One flash from my strobe and it rocketed off into the blue.

We swam toward the reef, coming across two gray angelfish. These disk-shaped fish are appropriately named, they're gray. Kimberly knelt on a bare patch of sand and held up one hand, snapping her fingers. Curious, the fish came in again and again to investigate as I took photos.

When I spotted a soft coral fan, I motioned Kimberly to swim over it, which she did several times. The scene, with the diver silhouetted in indigo water above the red branches of a gorgonian seafan, looked terrific on my camera's monitor.

Later, we saw a beautiful blue and yellow fish with a crown design on its head. Called a queen angel, it kept its distance.

All too soon, it was time to ascend. We made our way to the anchorline and kicked up alongside it, stopping at 15 feet for a three-minute safety stop.

At the dive platform, I handed my camera rig to the divemaster, then took off my fins and climbed aboard. Kimberly was right behind me. When she pulled her mask off she looked worried. "Sorry, Cinnamon," she said.

"Whatever for?"

"I tried not to but I must have scared that shark. And the queen angel just wouldn't let me close."

"It's not your fault, Kimberly. Those are wild animals," I said. "Sometimes they just aren't interested in being photographed. You were great."

Her face cleared. "I was?"

"Absolutely. I'm pretty sure I got some excellent shots. Let me dry off and I'll download the images to my computer so we can look at them."

Kimberly beamed.

Tom was fiddling with his tank near the stern. Although he scowled, he didn't say anything. I stowed my gear and rinsed off under the outdoor shower, then toweled myself dry before starting to work on my camera gear. Kimberly disappeared into the galley and came back with two warm, aromatic brownies. She handed one to me, then went back into the galley.

A moment later, Tom came by. Stopping only inches from me, he said in a low voice, "My wife doesn't dive with anyone but me, got that?"

"Your wife is an adult. She can dive with whomever she pleases," I replied.

"I won't tell you again," Tom said. "Mind your own damn business."

Chapter 4

The *DD II* came down hard, a body jarring experience that temporarily derailed my review of the past few days.

"Sorry about that, folks," Capt. Mac said. "Can somebody get me a bottle of water?"

Danny volunteered. I watched him pull himself to his feet while hanging onto the captain's seat, then make his way to the galley, bouncing from bulkhead to bulkhead like an errant Ping-Pong ball. He was back in a few minutes with three bottles. He handed one to the captain and one to me before lowering himself to the deck.

"You okay?" he asked.

"Fine," I said. I opened the bottle and took a long drink, remembering what had happened after Tom told me to mind my own business and stalked off.

Danny, on his way down the stairs from the sundeck, had witnessed the scene.

"What was that about?" he asked.

I told him what Tom had said, adding, "It sounded like a threat."

Danny frowned. "That S.O.B.," he said. He turned abruptly and headed for the galley door. Realizing what he had in mind, I grabbed his arm.

"Don't," I said. "He's a little guy with a big mouth. We're only stuck with him for a few more days. Let's just drop it."

Danny paused reluctantly. "I'd love to beat him to a bloody pulp," he said, pounding the fist of one hand into the palm of the other.

Mike and Dave came down the stairs from the sundeck in time to hear that.

"Don't tell me, let me guess who you're talking about," Mike said. "Could it be our beloved fellow passenger, Tom? What has he done now?"

"He threatened Cinnamon because she dived with Kimberly," Danny said.

"Big man," Mike said, contempt in his voice. "Picks on women. Amazon-like women such as Half-pint here."

"What did you do, Cinnamon?" Dave asked. "Pay The Mouse a compliment? Tom wouldn't want her to have any self-esteem, if she did she'd leave him."

And that, I thought, was the crux of the matter. I went below to my stateroom, where I changed into a dry swimsuit. I had learned the hard way that wearing a wet one all day could cause an itchy rash. Afterward I downloaded my photos to my laptop. They were every bit as good as I expected. Kimberly was graceful in the water and her dive gear was color coordinated. She'd done what I'd asked her to do and done it very well. Tom should be thrilled to have her as a model.

I made my way to the sundeck. As I passed the open door leading to the wheelhouse, Capt. Mac beckoned me inside. There, he patted the seat beside him. "Hop up," he said.

I did. The wheelhouse takes up the forward section of the bow on the sundeck and, since it is right off the captain's quarters, functions as his living room. There's a sofa on the port side. The captain's chair, with room for two, is right in front of the instrument panel. The latter is beneath three large windows offering a 180-degree view of the sea and contains every modern navigational device, including radar, GPS, color depth finder and more.

Captain Mac had both hands on the helm and as we talked his eyes scanned the sea, looking for dolphins. The second skipper leaned up against the instrument panel, eyes also constantly checking the seascape.

"I hear Tom made nasty to you and Danny wanted to bash him," Capt. Mac said.

"And I hear you nearly killed him last night," I replied.

"Yeah. I was going to choke him till his eyeballs popped out." Capt. Mac demonstrated by placing his hands around his own neck and shaking his head wildly.

The second skipper grinned. "You're quite the actor Mac," he said.

"Didn't win any awards last night," the captain continued. "I grab Tom and that little mouse doesn't scream, she just stands there, fiddling with that scarf she always wears. Twice I say, 'If someone doesn't stop me I'm gonna kill this sonofabitch.' Finally she gets the message and runs off to get help."

"You were just trying to scare Tom?"

Capt. Mac ran his fingers through his unruly hair. "Usually works," he said. "If people think I might beat the stuffin' out of 'em, they toe the line."

"Does this happen a lot?"

"Naw," Mac said, "hardly ever." He sounded disappointed. Then he changed the subject. "Did I show you these? I've got the world's cutest grandkids." He reached for the photo album resting atop the instrument panel. It contained more photos than any grandparent should be allowed to have. It was 15 minutes before I was able to get away. In the galley on the lower deck, I filled a plastic mug with ice-cold lemonade and carried it up to the sundeck. The pleasant scents of different sunscreens emanated from several inert bodies.

The sun was bright and the sky was clear and blue. It wouldn't be for long, though, dark clouds were gathering at the horizon.

I sank into a chaise lounge. I hadn't intended to nap, but the gentle rocking of the boat, the warmth of the sun and the soft breeze lulled me to sleep. Danny woke me about a half hour later. "Lunch is served, Sunshine," he said.

Since we were the last ones into the galley, we got stuck at the booth with Tom and The Mouse. She smiled nervously as we slid in; he didn't acknowledge us. The booths, in a row along the port side of the boat, are crescent shaped. This makes it difficult to converse with anyone but those sitting with you. Tom and Danny sat on the aisle ends, facing each other; The Mouse and I were side by side. Tom ignored us, staring out the window or down at his plate. We all ate quickly, eager to get away. As Danny and I were leaving, I gave Kimberly's hand a quick squeeze under the table. She returned it without meeting my eyes.

Chapter 5

Several hours later, we were still underway on horrendous seas. While things weren't any worse on our rocking boat, they weren't better, either. Waves slammed violently against the hull and white water came over the bow on a regular basis. I kept panic and terror at bay by staring at the opposite bulkhead as I remembered one very curious incident.

Late in the afternoon of our second day aboard the *DD II*, we were drifting on calm seas when two dolphins were seen heading our way. Mac announced this over the PA system, causing a collective groan to arise from the sundeck. We didn't mean to be ungrateful but we'd already had five or six incredible dolphin encounters that day. All that jumping into the water and swimming around, then climbing back on the boat, had worn us out.

"I can't do that again today," Jessica said. "I already feel like a drowned rat."

"The sun's so warm and comfy," Sandy said.

"I admit it, I'm way too lazy," Cathy said.

"I was just dozing off," Paul said.

Others murmured similar sentiments. Thus it was that only five people, including Danny and me, ended up in the water. To our surprise, the animals came right to us. Even more unexpected is that these weren't the spotted dolphins we had been seeing all day, they were bottlenoses. One came so close I touched it. It came even closer. As I patted its smooth, slippery body, the dolphin snuggled up to me.

I was thrilled beyond belief. I saw a notch on the animal's dorsal fin and decided to call it Notchy.

"Danny," I yelled, not taking my eyes off "my" dolphin.

"Look."

"Look at *me*," he replied. He and Dad were a few feet away, stroking the second dolphin while Tom shot photos.

The two animals kept up a continuous stream of clicks, whistles and squeaks.

"Cinnamon," Danny yelled. "You've got competition. Scratches loves me."

He had his arms around the dolphin. I tried embracing Notchy and was thrilled when the animal appeared to enjoy it.

We were very excited. The other dolphins we'd seen had always stayed just beyond reach.

I looked toward the boat. Captain Mac and the rest of the passengers were lined up along the railing, watching. It wasn't long before they joined us in the water.

Fourteen snorkelers trying to touch them spooked the dolphins. All too soon, they used their powerful tail flukes to disappear into the depths.

We swam back to the boat. As we climbed up on deck, an incredulous Captain Mac said, "I've been running dolphin trips for 20 years. Never got close a bottlenose. Never. Tried many times. And those animals let you touch them. Amazing. I have to wonder if they are escapees from a captive training program."

Where the dolphins came from didn't matter to us. "Danny and I hugged ours," I said, shivering at the thought of that fantastic event.

"That encounter alone was worth the price of the trip," Danny enthused. "I'll never forget it."

"It was the perfect way to end the day," I said.

"Does that mean you're not making the night dive?" Mac asked. "It's the Sugar Wreck again."

I considered this as I rinsed off under the deck shower. "I'll think about that later," I said. "After I'm dry and have had a snack."

Of course, even before dinner I knew I'd have to go. Last night's dive had been great and I'd heard there was plenty more to see on the site.

Danny and I made sure we were in the galley early for dinner so we could choose our booth mates. Dad and Sandy sat with us; Mike and Dave got stuck with Tom and The Mouse. They inhaled their meals and left. We understood; no one wanted to be around Tom any longer than necessary.

Only seven of us got ready for the night dive: Dave, Tom, Dad,

Paul, Pete, Danny and me. The divemaster hadn't been able to prevent Tom from diving alone the previous evening, but Mac stepped in tonight, insisting Tom go with buddy.

"We're in the middle of the ocean," he said. "Nobody goes in alone. You want to dive, you have to have a buddy."

Pete, who really wanted to dive with Paul and Dad, reluctantly agreed to go with Tom. Just before they jumped in I heard Tom giving Pete instructions. That, I knew, wouldn't sit well with the former marine, a long-time diver nearly 20 years his senior.

Again, we had a terrific dive. We found all sorts of creatures, including a large spider crab, a couple of southern stingrays, sleeping angelfish and pufferfish and schools of yellow striped French grunts. We didn't see the loggerhead until it was too late to take photos of it; my strobe battery was already dead.

Capt. Mac was standing on the stern when we climbed aboard.

"Surprise, surprise folks," he announced. "Guess who's not back yet."

"Tom," Danny and I chorused together.

"Is Pete here?" I asked. "You're damn right I am," Pete said, stepping out of the shadows. "The jerk disappeared about 10 minutes into the dive, while I was watching that big turtle. Don't know where he went. I came to the surface, like you're supposed to when you can't find your buddy, then went back down and searched for him. He was nowhere to be seen."

"You did the right thing," Danny said. "Tom probably ditched you on purpose. I wouldn't worry about it."

"I'm not gonna," Pete said. "Something happens to him it's his own damn fault."

While I went to our stateroom and took a hot shower, Danny went up on the sundeck to check out a comet that was supposed to be visible in the night sky. I was asleep when he returned.

Chapter 6

Hours passed. The skies remained an angry gray/black. No one spoke; we were tired and focused on surviving the storm on a boat that shuddered and shook from the impact of the waves and fierce winds. We seemed on the verge of capsizing or sinking on numerous occasions, yet the boat plodded on and on.

I thought back to Tom Tiburon's last day.

Right off the bat we noticed the cloud cover had thickened. There would be little sun that day. As had become my routine, I filled my mug with coffee in the galley and carried it upstairs to the sundeck. There, the two most important men in my life, my dad, Red Greene, and my boyfriend, Danny Decker, were stretched out in lounge chairs. Dad is just more than six feet tall and as lean as a string bean. Danny is a little taller, with a lot more muscle.

Some people fall in love gradually. Cupid's arrow hits me like a lightning bolt. I first set eyes on Danny on a California dive boat a year ago. Trim and buff, he was standing on the deck wearing only a blue swimsuit that matched the color of his eyes. When he saw me checking him out, he winked and grinned. I blushed. The bolt had struck. It was my good fortune that it hit Danny, too.

And now, here we were, on a boat in the Bahamas. When Danny saw me on the morning of Tom's last day he said, "You may be the only Sunshine we see today. I'm still amazed that you're up so early."

"Don't get used to it," I warned him, bending down to kiss the top of his curly brown head. I dragged a chair next to his and sank into it, careful not to spill my coffee.

"Mornin' Cinnamon," Dad said.

A baseball cap covered his gray-streaked red hair and he wore a green T-shirt with his store's logo on the sleeve.

I also work at Greene's One Stop Camera and Photo Shop, shooting portraits as well as making videos of weddings, Bar Mitzvahs, birthday and anniversary parties and any other rite of passage people want recorded for posterity. Greene's is the only full service photo shop in town; we sell batteries and camera equipment, including nearly every known digital accessory. We also produce color prints, calendars, mugs and other products from digital images.

"Did you see Sandy in the galley?" Dad asked.

"No," I said. "I don't think she's up yet."

"Not true," Sandy said, appearing at the top of the stairs. An oversized white T-shirt covered her yellow bikini. "Here I am."

I admit, I was jealous of Sandy at first. I'd had my dad all to myself for nearly three decades and it had never occurred to me I'd ever have to share him. Yet here he was, dating a smart, funny and very attractive woman my age.

Maybe I wasn't as grown-up about that as I could have been.

Sandy had her own issues. She didn't mind that her boyfriend had an adult daughter until I moved back to Cliffview and was suddenly in their life full time. Both of us loved Dad, however, and it didn't take long for me to see how happy he was and her to figure out I'd make a better friend than an enemy.

Now Sandy and I are good friends. I was her maid of honor when she and Dad married last winter and she's about to produce a sibling for me, something I've always wanted but never thought I'd get. Better late than never.

This morning, Sandy wore a broad brimmed hat over her cap of short shiny blond hair and her blue eyes were hidden behind mirrored sunglasses. She kissed Dad on the cheek, then pulled a chair next to his and sat down, holding her mug in both hands.

We sipped coffee in companionable silence for several minutes as the crew started the engines. Diesel fumes wafted upward, then dispersed as the anchor was pulled and the boat got underway.

Sandy turned to Danny. "Have I told you how much I love this trip?"

Danny laughed. "Not today. But I think you mentioned it 10 or 20 times yesterday."

"We all love this trip," a voice said. I knew whose it was without looking. "Too bad we can't say the same about everyone who's on it."

Mike dragged a chair over to our little group. Dave was behind him, wearing his hat-of-the-day, a jaunty green number with a red feather stuck in the band.

"Don't your wives object to you going off without them?" I asked.

"Heck, no, they encourage us," Mike replied.

"The Lovely Laura thinks our trips should be longer," Dave added.

"I walk in the door from a trip, Burgie starts asking when I'm leaving on the next," Mike said.

"The Lovely Laura surfs the 'net for us," Dave said. "'Oh, honey,' she says, 'Diving with great white sharks in South Africa. Doesn't that sound exciting? Your life insurance is paid up, isn't it, sweetheart?'"

"Burgie thinks we should go to Antarctica," Mike said. "She's found a trip for us that lasts six months."

Jessica Wheeler arrived during this latter exchange. "I've heard there are lots of guys and very few women down there," she commented.

"Not my cup of tea," Paul said as he came up the stairs with Cathy. Although still far from slim, he'd lost some weight recently and, missing that insulation, was no longer as impervious to cold water as he used to be. He'd been complaining about that on our Wednesday Warrior dive trips in California.

Cathy shivered. "I'm definitely a warm water wuss," she admitted. "I wouldn't even consider putting so much as a toe in Antarctica's icy ocean."

"You're all wusses," came a voice from the stairwell. "Disgusting, chicken-livered wusses. I, on the other hand, am a manly man. Not afraid of a little cold water." Pete strutted out on the deck and struck a classic pose in front of us in swim trunks and T-shirt, one hand on his hip, the other flexing a bicep.

"Put a cork in it," Paul advised his friend cheerfully. "California waters are warmer than Antarctica's yet you wear a drysuit with heat packs in it. You're just as wimpy as the rest of us."

"So much for my manly image," Pete said. He pulled a chair up alongside me. Before he could sit down, however, the last two members of our group, Tom and Kimberly, appeared on the sundeck.

Pete headed downstairs immediately. The rest of us followed. Two days ago someone would have felt guilty about being so rude and uttered an excuse, today several people glared openly at Tom. I felt sorry for The Mouse, who lowered her eyes and chewed on her upper lip.

Since breakfast was imminent, most of us found seats in the galley. Paul and Cathy, along with Pete and his girlfriend, Jessica, settled into one booth, Sandy, Dad, Danny and me in another.

When Mike and Dave arrived, they took seats in the empty booth.

Then Tom and Kimberly walked in. There were only two seats left and they were in Mike and Dave's booth. As soon as they sat down, Mike and Dave stood up.

Mike came over to our booth. "Any chance I could squeeze in with you guys? I had the privilege of eating breakfast and dinner with the world famous photographer yesterday. Wouldn't want to hog all his valuable time."

No one replied, we just moved closer together. Mike slid in next to me.

Dave slid into the booth next to Jessica. That left one entire booth just for the Tiburons.

Dad said, "He doesn't bother me that much. I'll sit with him."

"You enjoyed the lecture he gave you yesterday on how to take photos?" I asked. "You were taking U/W photos before he was born."

"I'm not that old, honey," Dad objected. He stood up and carried his coffee mug over to Tom and Kimberly's booth.

"I'll join you," Danny said. There was some shuffling of people before we were all settled again.

Tom smiled. "New table-mates," he said, sounding pleased. "Good. Eating every meal with a pair of faggots gets old fast."

I felt Mike stiffen but when I glanced at him, his face was impassive. Dave, on the other hand, turned bright red.

Danny and Dad looked at each other, then slipped out of the booth.

"You've got to be the biggest jackass I've ever met," Danny told Tom. "I hope to God I never see you again when this trip is over." He grabbed his mug and headed for my table. Dad did, too.

Tom frowned. "You can fool some of the people some of the time," he quoted darkly.

Just then the cook announced breakfast was ready. While we didn't know it then, it was the last breakfast anyone would ever have to share with Tom Tiburon.

Chapter 7

It's hard to sit in one place on a wildly rocking boat. I leaned back against the bulkhead and planted my feet firmly on the deck in front of me. Then I thought back to the third morning of our trip.

As we breakfasted on carrot/raisin/bran muffins, spinach-cheese omelets, fresh fruit and whole wheat toast, the boat traveled to the first dive site and the topic of conversation turned to underwater photography.

"Danny loves it when I shoot close-ups," I said. "He's good at finding little critters. But he hates modeling. I make him point his toes."

"I don't hate it," Danny explained. "It's just not all that much fun. Besides, Cinnamon is a tyrant behind the camera."

"I am not," I objected.

"Yes you are," Dad said. "She even makes *me* point my toes."

"I could try posing for you, Cinnamon," Jessica offered. "If one of the pictures turned out okay, maybe you could have a print made for me."

"Now there's a great idea," Danny said.

"Offer accepted," I said. "Now let me see you point your toes." Everyone laughed.

After breakfast, I went outside to work on my camera gear. Underwater photography is equipment and maintenance intensive. There's always something to do. Dad and Tom were also at the camera table, working on their rigs.

Although I hadn't said as much to anyone, I thought Pete and Jessica an odd couple. Pete, a widower in his early 60s, had taught boys' PE at Cliffview High for many years, including the three I was there. He had retired recently. Tall and angular, he had brown eyes, tanned, leathery skin and a bristly gray crew cut. He'd served in the U.S. Marine Corps right out of high school and had their distinctive emblem tattooed on one arm.

Jessica, quiet and shy, was in her early 40s. Nearly as tall as Pete, she had straight, shoulder length light brown hair. She seemed self-conscious about her height and always stood hunched over. Her eyes were hazel and her face was neither pretty nor ugly, just plain.

After I finished getting my cameras ready, we went into the galley and I gave Jessica a few tips on modeling.

Once the boat was anchored over Cerro Reef, the divemaster gave his usual briefing, using a hand drawn diagram of the site. Jess and I geared up and reviewed hand signals before jumping in.

Cerro Reef was a seamount that began about 55 feet below the surface. It had abundant fish life and lots of bright orange elephant ear sponges, some of which were several feet wide. These sponges are fairly flat and have irregular shapes.

The 82°F water was clear, with visibility of at least 100 feet.

A bit awkward on land, Jessica was surprisingly graceful underwater. Her slender body looked terrific in a blue wetsuit with yellow accent panels. Her fins, snorkel and mask were blue.

We finished the dive with some sightseeing and ascended along the anchorline, making a three-minute safety stop at 15 feet before surfacing.

"You were super, Jess," I said as we climbed up on the dive ramp. "So graceful."

Jessica smiled. "That was fun," she said. "I'll be happy to model for you any time."

"Wonderful," I said. "Danny will enjoy the break. And I'll have some prints made for you. I've already got several shots I think you'd be proud to hang on your wall."

Jessica's smile widened, revealing small, even and bright white teeth.

After our gear was stowed, we rinsed off under the warm water shower on the deck and dried ourselves with warm towels from a basket.

I put on a T-shirt and wrapped a towel around my head. Just then the cook came out of the galley carrying a plate of freshly baked chocolate chip cookies. I grabbed two and found them delicious. As I was retrieving my camera rig from the freshwater rinse tank, I saw The Mouse come out of the galley.

31

"The shots I took of you yesterday look very nice," I told her. "Would you like to see them?"

She glanced behind her before answering. "Not right now," she said. "Tom was really upset about that. He says I'll learn bad habits working with another photographer."

"He also said you're a terrible model," I said. "He's trying to lower your self-esteem. Don't let him get away with it."

She started to say something but Tom came out of the galley just then so she turned and went up the stairs to the sundeck. Tom glared at me before following her.

I went back to work on my camera gear. Jessica came out of the galley and stood next to me.

"I need your help with something," she said hesitantly.

"Anything for my best model."

"I've been using this little camera to take pictures," she said. "But the photos are way too dark."

A few minutes later we were seated at one of the booths in the galley, where I transferred Jessica's first attempts at underwater photography to my laptop.

We were viewing the images when Tom walked by. He stopped and peered over our shoulders.

"Those are just dreadful, Cinnamon."

"They're not hers, they're mine," Jessica said.

"They're still dreadful," Tom said. "Do yourself a favor, Jess, don't waste any more of your paltry salary pursuing photography. You have no talent."

Tears appeared in Jessica's eyes but the next few words out her mouth surprised me. "Screw you, asshole," she said.

"You, screw me? Fat chance," Tom retorted, deliberately misunderstanding what she'd said. Then he went on through the galley.

Chapter 8

I knew we hadn't been on a boat for decades, trying to outrun a hurricane, but it sure felt as if we had. Everyone was exhausted. Even Capt. Mac's usually perky moustache was drooping. I didn't want to know he might be getting discouraged. To keep my mind off the present, I thought back to our last snorkel.

The few hours after lunch were always the laziest part of a day on the *DD II*. We'd get our cameras and snorkeling gear ready, then sit around chatting, reading or getting some sun, keeping an eye out for dolphins, which were rarely sighted during this time.

It was nearly 3:00 when the first pod was spotted. Capt. Mac uttered the familiar words and we rushed to get ready. When the divemaster yelled, "Go, go, go!" I jumped in and swam toward the dolphins. Danny was right behind me.

On our previous encounters, the dolphins hadn't stopped they'd simply looked at us and continued on by. Snorkelers trailed them, kicking furiously in their attempts to keep up with the sleek, spotted animals. The sight reminded me of a slow car on a two-lane country road with a line of autos behind it.

This time, however, five dolphins slowed as they approached Danny and me, then stopped altogether. I started taking photos as the animals milled around us. I shot three dolphins together, nearly nose to nose with Danny, and I shot them swimming by, eyeing me curiously.

A parent and child pair captivated me. The baby stayed close to its mother, who kept her body between us. I took several photos of the baby peeking shyly at me.

Danny, wearing only swimsuit, fins, mask and snorkel had an inspiration. He dived underwater and did a somersault. To our delight, when he repeated the trick after surfacing for a breath of air, the mother and baby joined him. The acrobatics were repeated three or four times.

Later, floating face down on the surface, we watched several dolphins. They played keep-away with a strand of sargassum grass; they swam upside down; they hung head down in the water; they stood on their flukes just above the sand. They glanced at us frequently to make sure we were appreciating the show. A couple of animals rooted in the sand with their beaks, digging up what looked like sand tilefish and eating them. All of the activities were carried out silently. There weren't any of the clicks and squeaks I had expected.

I wanted this magical encounter to last forever.

That was not to be. While five dolphins were entertaining Danny and me, the rest of our group was having its own encounter with nine others. When those dolphins disappeared into the blue, ten people descended upon our little pod.

Five dolphins and 12 people in one small area created chaos. Tom started barking instructions at The Mouse, who was trying to pose with the animals. That was nearly impossible; the dolphins were moving, as were all of people in the water with them.

"Stupid," Tom yelled at his wife. The next word out of his mouth was, "Clumsy." Kimberly finally succeeded in getting nose to beak with one of the animals. Before Tom could trigger the shutter, Pete swam into the picture. Tom lost his temper.

"Get out of the frickin' way, idiot!" he screamed. "Everybody, get out of the way."

The humans weren't the only ones who didn't like the ruckus. The dolphins were gone in seconds. We didn't see them again that day, although we spent another couple of hours looking.

Everyone was outraged. Mike and Pete wanted to lock Tom in his stateroom for the duration of the trip. Danny, acting as peacemaker, pointed out we'd only be stuck with Tom for another three days, then he'd be out of our lives, hopefully forever.

While we couldn't imprison him, we didn't have to be nice to Tom. With the exception of his wife, everyone on board pointedly ignored him.

Since no one wanted to sit with them, the Tiburons had a booth all to themselves at dinner time and the rest of us crowded into the remaining three. I felt sorry for Kimberly, whose downcast eyes and frown telegraphed her unhappiness. When Tom left before she finished her dessert, I joined her.

"It's not you we have an issue with," I told her.

"I know," she said, not looking at me.

"Three more days," I reminded her. "Then this nightmare will be over."

"For you, maybe," she said. "Not for me."

Once again, we anchored for the night dive over the Sugar Wreck. I had seen things on my other two dives that I hadn't gotten to photograph and was looking forward to this one. Danny and Dad were equally enthusiastic about the dive. Everyone else pleaded fatigue. Everyone, that is, except Tom. As Dad, Danny and I were getting ready to go in the water, he came out on the deck.

I had wondered why Capt. Mac was hanging around; he usually spent the latter part of each evening relaxing in the galley, watching a movie on DVD. Now, as Tom walked over to his gear storage bin, the captain stepped in front of him.

"You are not going into the water tonight," he said.

"The hell I'm not," Tom replied.

"You ignored the rules the last two nights," Capt. Mac said. "You'll sit this one out."

"Who's going to make me?" Tom asked, a smirk on his face.

"We are," Capt. Mac said. The divemaster and second skipper came out of the shadows and stood beside him. The three of them stared down at Tom.

There was total silence for a couple of minutes before Tom turned on his heels and walked into the galley.

"Poor Kimberly," I said.

"When you marry an asshole, you have to expect shit," Mac said.

Our third dive on the Sugar Wreck was as eventful as the first two. I took several shots of the big loggerhead turtle and Dad shot extensive video.

Our dive lasted an hour. The divemaster logged us in and went off to bed before 9:30 for the first time that week. I plugged my battery chargers into an electrical outlet before joining Danny in our stateroom. Except for the hum of the generator the boat was quiet. Everyone seemed to have settled in for the evening.

Chapter 9

I was so engrossed in my memories of the earlier days of our trip that I almost forgot where I was. The thunderous noise of a spectacular wave crashing over the bow and windshield brought me briefly back to the present. Then I continued my reverie.

The morning after the captain refused to let Tom night dive, the boat was underway and we were eating breakfast when The Mouse walked through the galley. She frowned when she passed the empty booth we'd left for her and Tom and continued on out to the deck. A few minutes later she was back. Standing in the doorway she asked, "Has anyone seen Tom? I can't find him."

A chorus of "nos," answered her.

"Ask Mac to page him," I suggested.

She went through the galley to the wheelhouse, where the captain and crew were having their breakfast. We heard her talking to someone but couldn't hear what she said. Capt. Mac's reaction, however, was loud and clear.

"That sonofabitch better not have gone in the water last night," he exclaimed. "Not after I told him not to."

We heard Kimberly protest, "All of his gear and cameras are on board."

The captain got on the PA, "Tom Tiburon, get your ass into the wheelhouse."

We went back to our breakfasts.

When Tom still hadn't made an appearance five minutes later, the captain made a second announcement. "Tom Tiburon, see me in the wheelhouse. Now."

Danny and I looked at each other, an identical thought in our minds. We slid out of the booth and went out on the deck. We were staring at Tom's tank when the captain, divemaster and The Mouse arrived.

The tank was set up for a dive, with BC and regulator attached. The captain picked up the regulator high-pressure hose and looked at the air-integrated computer on the end of it. Next he lifted the lid of the bench seat below the tank. Inside were Tom's mask, snorkel and fins.

"His tank is full," Capt. Mac said, "and none of his gear is missing. He didn't make a dive last night."

"Both of his camera systems are here, too," I said.

"Sonofabitch," the captain swore. He strode toward the wheelhouse and a few minutes later, addressed us over the PA.

"Good morning, folks. We're gonna search the boat in a few minutes. Please stay in the galley till we finish. Have another cup of coffee and relax."

The captain and divemaster started the search below decks. Not long afterward, they came through the galley and went outside. Soon, they were back in the galley.

"Tom isn't on the boat," Capt. Mac told us. He addressed the The Mouse. "When did you see him last?"

"About 9:30," she said. "I haven't been sleeping well, so I took a pill. I didn't wake up till daybreak."

"And what was Tom doing when you went to bed?" the captain asked.

The Mouse wouldn't look at him and didn't answer right away. Finally she glanced at him sidewise and said, "He was getting ready to make the night dive."

"How'd he get by night watch?" The captain demanded, barely containing his temper.

The second skipper, who had been on night watch, turned bright red. "Kimberly was worried another boat might run into us in the dark so I showed her how the radar works. He must have gone into the water then."

Kimberly kept her eyes on the deck.

Mac sighed loudly before asking, "Anybody see Tom after 9:30 last night?"

There was a chorus of "nos."

"Sonofabitch," the captain said. He headed toward the wheelhouse. A few minutes later the boat made a wide circle and headed back to the Sugar Wreck. In the wheelhouse Danny and I listened as the captain called the Miami Sector of the United States Coast Guard, notifying them that one of his passengers was missing and presumed overboard. They would let the Royal Bahamas Defence Force (RBDF) and the Bahamas Air Sea Rescue Association (BASARA) know we needed their help.

Chapter 10

On the morning Tom went missing there was no sun at all; dark clouds covered the sky and there was a freshening breeze. We learned more about the weather through the exchanges between the captain and the rescue agencies that day.

The tropical depression once stalled in the Atlantic was on the move and increasing in intensity. It was expected to be reclassified as a tropical storm and could pass through the Bahamas within 36 hours.

We wouldn't be diving anymore. Mac advised us to get ready for a really bumpy ride. The crew scurried about, stowing or tying down everything. The passengers packed dive gear and personal items and secured our luggage as best we could in our staterooms.

We had finished doing that when first RBDF boats arrived. Three planes belonging to volunteers from BASARA soon followed. The peace and quiet of the previous days was replaced with the buzz of the planes and the sound of boat engines. In the wheelhouse, we listened while those in the air and on the sea communicated with each other via radio.

By then we were once again over the Sugar Wreck. The wind had picked up and the swells had become waves. It was too dangerous to anchor in the shallow water over the wreck so Mac dropped his divemaster and Danny (the only two search and rescue certified divers on board) in the water near the wreck before motoring a short distance away to wait while they scoured the site with four RBDF divers.

The men disappeared beneath the surface and didn't return until they'd exhausted their air supplies an hour later. We knew they hadn't found anything as soon as we saw their faces.

"There is a lot of surge and everything's all stirred up," Danny said as he climbed onto the bouncing dive platform and pulled off his facemask. "So much sand in the water that visibility is only a couple of inches. We could have passed right over a body and not seen it."

There was intermittent rain. Passengers and crew lined the railings, eyes scanning the seas, looking for the vanished member of our group. There were several false sightings. Hopes rose and fell like the seas.

During the time we'd spent on the boat, Tom had irritated everyone. Many of us silently rehearsed the scathing words we'd utter when we plucked him from the ocean. He was an experienced diver; everyone thought he'd be found alive.

As the day wore on and there was no sign of him, however, anger turned to concern and concern to fear.

All activity ceased in the late afternoon. Before they left, the search and rescue teams told us the worsening weather would prevent them from returning the next day. Dinner was a somber affair, minus the chatter and camaraderie that had marked our meals on other days.

Capt. Mac wanted to make one more underwater search first thing in the morning. Then he intended to head for Miami well ahead of the approaching storm. He anchored the *DD II* on a deep site and we spent an uneasy night on seas that grew rougher and rougher. Many passengers became seasick. Finding their cabins too claustrophobic, they tried to sleep curled up in galley booths or on the sofa or deck in the wheelhouse.

Danny and were tossed around in the bunk in our cabin and barely slept. I didn't feel refreshed when I awoke.

I don't think Capt. Mac slept at all. Of the people on board, he was the most upset about Tom's disappearance, considering it a personal affront.

"I've never lost a diver in the 20 years I've been running these trips," he announced to no one in particular on several occasions. "Never had a serious injury. I knew his reputation. I never should have left Miami with that sonofabitch on my boat."

It was when the *Dolphin Diver II* began her return trip to Miami that the dolphins brought Tom to us.

Chapter 11

Reliving the days we spent on the boat before Tom went missing had occupied me on the rough trip back to Miami. We were 30 minutes from the Florida coast when we heard good news over the radio: The hurricane was rapidly losing strength. Even better, it had taken a sudden turn to the northeast. Other than several power outages, some wind damage and relatively minor flooding, the Bahamas had been spared its full wrath.

The skies remained dark, though the wind, rain and swells diminished a bit.

A cheer went up in the wheelhouse when Capt. Mac announced, "Land ho!"

There, in the distance was Miami. Some of us wept tears of joy.

When the boat finally motored into the much calmer waters of the marina, the recovery of the seasick was immediate and miraculous. Cacophony reigned as cell phones sprouted in nearly every hand and passengers roamed the boat telling loved ones about our adventures.

Captain Mac had expected the boat to be met by Coast Guard personnel and a local coroner but their workload was extra heavy because of the storm and it would be hours before they could take a report and remove Tom's body.

Mac had arranged hotel rooms for his passengers and taxis were waiting to take us there. Danny and I went below to bring up our luggage. As we passed Mike and Dave's stateroom, Danny bent over and retrieved a scrap of paper from the deck. He rolled it into a ball and, inside our room, threw it at the wastebasket. He missed.

"Let a pro do it, Danny," I said. "I wasn't the star pitcher of the Cliffview High girls' softball team for nothing."

"It won't stay rolled up," Danny warned me. He picked up the paper, made a ball of it and tried to toss it to me.

This throw was also short; the paper fell to the deck in front of me and began unrolling. When I stooped to pick it up, I noticed writing on it. The paper was unusually thick and had a glossy finish. A couple of sentences had been neatly printed on it in blue ink. Because it was torn, only two words were legible. Danny came up next to me and peered over my shoulder. "Something, something 'blame me,' something, something," he read.

The other side of the scrap was blank.

"What the hell is that supposed to mean?" Danny asked.

"Don't know," I said.

Just then someone yelled. "Taxis are waiting folks."

I stuffed the paper into a jeans pocket and grabbed a couple of bags. It took us several trips to get everything into our taxi and we got drenched in the process. The wind was still incredibly strong; if I hadn't been weighted down with heavy luggage, I might have been blown off my feet.

My last photo case was wedged under the camera table on the deck of the *DD II*. When I pulled it out, a little red and white pen rolled out. I'd seen it before, it was the pen from Dave's logbook. I picked it up and put it in my purse, thinking I'd return it to Dave at the hotel.

Danny and I were saying good-bye to the crew in the wheelhouse when Mike came in. His face was white, his eyes looked wild.

"I can't find Dave," he said.

"Oh no," I said. I felt as if I'd been punched in the stomach.

"Aw shit," Mac said, rubbing his eyes.

"Maybe he already left in a taxi," Danny suggested.

"He wouldn't do that without telling me," Mike said. "Besides, all his stuff is still in our stateroom."

"Let's not panic," Mac said. "We'll search the boat. Maybe he fell asleep somewhere." He yelled to his crew and, when they'd gathered in the wheelhouse, issued orders. Danny, Mike and I started on the top deck and worked our way down. Mac, the second skipper and divemaster started in the engine room and worked their way up. We met in the galley.

A look at everyone's faces told the story: Dave wasn't on board. Mac wasn't ready to give up, though.

"When did you see him last?" he asked.

"He was in a booth in the galley just after we got Tom on board," I said.

"He was still in the galley when I went to our stateroom about an hour later," Mike said. "He wasn't moving around much, he was too seasick."

"I don't remember when I saw him last," Danny admitted.

"Damn," Mac said, expressing the dismay we all felt with the understatement of the week. "You know we can't go back out there," he told Mike. "No one can go out there right now."

Mike nodded, tears forming in his eyes. "He's my best friend," he said.

"I'll report him missing," the captain said. "That's all I can do."

We were passing through the galley when a thought popped in to my head.

"Did anyone check the walk-in freezer?"

Danny and Mike looked at me as if I were insane.

"Tom's in there," Danny said.

Mac said, "We didn't look in there on account of the body. We'll look now." He strode to the big stainless steel door and yanked it open.

Inside the freezer, opposite Tom's black plastic covered body, Dave lay on his side in a fetal position, white and lifeless. He wore only swim trunks.

I covered my mouth with my hands to stifle a scream.

"Holy Mother of Christ," Mac said.

The cold air hit us as we stared at the gruesome tableau. Then Mike sprang forward.

"Dave, Dave," he cried. He grabbed one of Dave's arms and tried pulling him out of the freezer. The body was frozen in place.

"You can't help him," Mac said. "Leave him be. He's dead." He took Mike's arm, led him out of the freezer and closed the door.

"Could Dave have gotten trapped in there accidentally?" I asked.

Mac let go of Mike and turned around. He went into the freezer, closing the door behind him. I sucked in a breath. Seconds later, the door opened and Mac stepped out. "As you can see, the inside latch is working," he said.

Chapter 12

Mac had called the Coast Guard to say that instead of one, there were two bodies in his freezer.

Since he used his cell phone, we were only able to hear his side of the conversation:

"Don't know how he died. It looks as if he's been in there awhile."

"No problem. We weren't going to clean the boat till tomorrow anyway."

"Only three are here, the rest of them are at a hotel. It was a hell of a trip. They could hardly wait to get off the boat. We found the second body after they'd left."

"Yeah, I know where they're staying."

"One victim's luggage is here but the other's wife took his, I helped her put it in the taxi."

"Okay. I'm going to lock the boat up and go home. Call when you're ready and I'll meet you here."

After saying good-bye to Mac, Mike, Danny and I made the trip to the hotel in silence through dark, near empty and oft flooded streets. The driver had his hands full keeping his wind and rain buffeted taxi on the road.

Dave's death had shaken me to my very soul. He was so nice, so funny and now, so dead. It didn't make any sense. How had he ended up in the freezer with a man he despised?

It was late when we arrived at the hotel. It was dark, with only candles lighting the lobby because power in the city had been off for several hours. There were only a few guests and a skeleton crew.

After checking in, Danny and I showered together in the flickering light of several candles. The water wasn't hot but that didn't matter, it felt heavenly anyway. Danny shampooed my hair. I loved the way it smelled and how squeaky clean it felt when he finished.

Later, as I bent over the sink to brush my teeth for the first time in two days, the floor seemed to rock gently, as it always did after several days at sea.

The next thing Danny and I wanted was food.

"I don't think I've ever been so hungry," I said, dressing hastily in a clean T-shirt and shorts.

"I would even eat peas," Danny said. He hated peas.

We used one of our underwater flashlights to navigate the dark hallways to the coffee shop. There, we found Dad, Sandy, Pete, Jess, Cathy and Paul sitting at a candlelit table. In the center was a platter of plastic-wrapped sandwiches, a bowl containing small bags of chips and another full of apples, oranges and bananas. Bottled water rounded out the selection.

"We saved a place for you, honey," Dad said, "but we were beginning to worry. We've already finished eating. Where have you been?"

"We ran into a problem," I said.

"Where are Mike and Dave?" Paul asked.

Danny devoured two sandwiches while I told the group about Dave. "We don't know how he got in the freezer or exactly when," I said, finishing my story.

Even in the dim light, I could see shock on the faces around me. Sandy moved closer to Dad, who put an arm around her.

"All I know about the last couple days is that I was so sick I wanted to die," she said.

Several others nodded in agreement.

"I remember seeing Dave in the galley," Pete said. "I just don't remember when. The last few days have run together in my mind."

"I saw him in the galley, too," Dad said. "Several times. I have no idea when I saw him last."

I grabbed two sandwiches and ate them, not caring what they were. The group began to disperse before I finished. A bag of Fritos and an apple later, Danny and I headed back to our room through dark, empty halls.

Danny collapsed on our bed and fell asleep almost instantly. I brushed my teeth again and blew out the candles. The air in the room was hot and humid and I could hear the wind howling outside. Yet as soon as my head hit the pillow I was out.

I slept deeply, awakening to the hum of air conditioning and a much cooler room. Danny was fully dressed and sitting in a chair by the plywood covered window. He seemed lost in thought.

"How's the weather?" I asked.

Danny started and said, "The worst is over. The power's back on."

"Have you had breakfast?" I asked.

"Just a cup of coffee. I was waiting for you."

Coffee, nice hot coffee. That got me out of bed.

On the "Daily Special" board in the coffee shop someone had printed, "Good-bye Hurricane Harry!"

I lingered at the buffet, where the hot food smelled and looked so good, before putting a large scoop of scrambled eggs on my plate, along with three slices of bacon and a blueberry-bran muffin. I carried my plate over to the table where several members of our group sat.

"Mornin' Cinnamon," several people chorused as I hustled off to get a cup of coffee.

"You look a lot better," I said to Sandy as I set my cup down next to Danny. Sandy's hair was clean and shiny; there was color in her cheeks. Her plate contained four slices of French toast, drenched in maple syrup.

"She is lots better," Dad agreed with a smile, kissing his wife's cheek. "And she's making up for all the meals she couldn't eat on the boat."

Kimberly arrived and sat down next to me, then busied herself eating. One by one, the rest of the group joined us.

The group got quiet when Mike appeared. None of us knew what to say to him. He ate quickly and left. Kimberly followed soon after. Neither said anything at all to anybody.

After breakfast, we drifted off to the lobby, drawn by the sounds of plywood being removed from the hotel's ground floor windows. There we could see conditions were greatly improved. The wind was considerably lighter and the rain came intermittently. Danny and I went back to our room, where we watched the news on TV. Afterward, I picked up the Laura Lippman novel I'd been reading on the *DD II*. I fell asleep after a few pages.

When I awoke, I went to the lobby, where I found Danny talking to Cathy, Paul, Dad and Sandy.

"We were just about to eat lunch," he said.

"Great," I said. "I'm hungry again."

By the time we finished lunch, the rain had stopped and rays of sun had broken through the cloud cover. The maintenance crew had begun cleaning up the palm fronds, tree branches and debris that covered the hotel grounds. There were puddles of water everywhere.

We had spent many days confined to a small area. I was restless. I suggested a walk to Danny and he readily agreed. Several other people decided to come along. When Danny and I started off down a two-lane road littered with storm detritus, they followed.

We set a brisk pace on purpose and soon outdistanced the others. When I was sure we were out of earshot, I asked, "What do you think happened to Dave?"

Danny shrugged. "I have no idea."

"Well," I said. "I think his death is connected to Tom's murder."

"Murder?" Danny said, "What makes you think it was murder?"

"Tom's neck was bruised. He was strangled. That's why I took photos of his body."

"How do you know those marks weren't made after he died?"

"There wouldn't have been any bruising if they were made after death. I think whoever killed Tom also murdered Dave. Maybe because he knew too much."

Danny stared at me. "Two murders? Come on, Cinnamon. There were two tragic accidents on our trip. Nobody was murdered. That forensic photographer job has made you paranoid."

"Dad, Sandy, Paul, Cathy, you and me are definitely not involved," I said, ignoring him. "That leaves the boat crew, along with Pete, Jessica, The Mouse and Mike." I ticked off the suspects on my fingers.

"Your imagination is working overtime, Cinnamon," Danny said. "You're seeing things that aren't there. There haven't been any murders. There aren't any suspects. Period."

"Do you think Dave just walked into the freezer and sat down?" I asked.

"How the hell would I know?" Danny was yelling now. "He was seasick. Maybe he went in there by mistake and couldn't get out."

"That's ridiculous, Danny. Mac showed us the inside latch is working. Somebody put Dave there before or after they murdered him."

"I don't want to hear any more half-baked theories about

murder," Danny said. He took off, leaving me standing alone.

I heard voices behind me; the group was approaching. I didn't feel like talking to any of them, not even Dad. I broke into a jog. Avoiding all the puddles and stuff on the road required total concentration. I ran until I could run no longer, finally slowing to a walk. The others were out of sight behind me; Danny was nowhere to be seen in front of me. I turned around and started back.

I thought about Tom's death. Nobody liked him but why would anyone kill him? The trip was half over; Tom would have been out of everyone's life in a few days. Everyone except The Mouse, that is. I didn't consider her a suspect, however. In my estimation, she lacked the physical and mental strength to strangle her husband. She was, after all, a mouse, small and timid.

Then there was Dave. Unless he'd seen something he shouldn't have, I couldn't think why anyone would want to harm him. He was well liked, except by Tom, of course, but Tom was already dead when Dave died, murdered, I was sure, by whoever killed Tom.

Chapter 13

Back at the hotel, I was in for an unpleasant surprise; Danny had moved out of our room. That sent an arrow through my heart. I called the front desk and asked for him. The clerk wouldn't give me Danny's room number. I used my cell phone to call him. When there was no answer, I left a message asking him to call me. Then I turned on my laptop and spent the next few hours answering emails and doing other work related computer chores.

I was just putting the laptop away when there was a knock on the door. I was hoping for Danny when I answered it. My spirits fell when I saw it was Dad.

"Hey honey," he said. "Sandy has this incredible craving for pizza. Want to come with us?"

"I better check with Danny."

"He's already left. He, Jess and Pete are meeting an old buddy of Pete's for dinner. Danny suggested we call you," Dad added. "He didn't think you had any plans."

I mulled that over for a few seconds. Another arrow through the heart.

"Honey?" Dad said at last.

"I'll be ready in ten. Meet you in the lobby."

I didn't think I was all that hungry until the extra large black olive and sausage pizza arrived. It looked and smelled fantastic. I do believe it was the best pizza I have ever had. I ate almost as much as Sandy, who was eating for two.

"So what's up with you and Danny?" Dad asked when we'd polished off the last piece of crispy crust.

"I'm not sure."

"You must have some idea," Sandy said. "Did you have a fight? We saw him moving his stuff to another room. He wouldn't tell us why."

"You don't have to talk about it if you don't want to," Dad said, always one to avoid confrontations and unpleasantness.

"Oh yes, she does," Sandy said. "Spit it out, Cinnamon."

I felt my cheeks redden. "I guess he just needs some time alone. There is such a thing as too much togetherness."

"Yeah, right," Sandy said. "Let me know when you're ready to talk."

Back at the hotel, everyone but me was surprised to find that two Miami-Dade police officers had been looking for us. When the ten of us were finally together in the lobby, they told us they needed to interview each of us about the deaths of Tom and Dave. They took us to a small conference room on the second floor. Each person would be interviewed separately.

We awaited our turns uneasily. Some read, others watched TV. There was no idle chitchat.

I spent some of my time studying my fellow travelers.

Kimberly and Mike were the only ones who didn't look well rested. Both had dark circles under their eyes. Most of us had showered, delighted to remove salt and for many, the reminders they'd been seasick. Kimberly had obviously done so. Her hair was clean and pulled back into a ponytail. She was neatly dressed in a clean, pale blue T-shirt and navy blue shorts. There was a dark blue silk scarf around her neck.

Mike, however, still had on the rumpled maroon shorts and stained green T-shirt he'd worn for the past few days. His hair was crusty with dried salt from sea spray and stuck up at odd angles. He seemed restless, alternately drumming his fingers on the arm of his chair and jiggling one foot. I walked over and sat down next to him. He didn't reply when I said, "Hi, how are you?" so I put my hand on his arm. He gave me a startled look. His eyes were bloodshot.

"Mike," I said in a low voice. "How are you?"

"Not good," he mumbled.

"Want to talk about it?" I asked.

"No," he said, shaking my hand off.

Before I had a chance to say more, he was summoned to his interview.

After he left, I found a pad of paper and a pen on a table next to a phone and composed a timetable of the trip, complete with what I considered important events. That kept me busy for the rest of my wait, which was considerable because I was last person interviewed. Once they left the room I was in, nobody returned and I was alone there for more than an hour.

Finally, it was my turn.

The detective who interviewed me, Storm Gray, looked exhausted. He had a video camera set up on a tripod and asked if I minded my interview being recorded. Of course I said "No."

After we got the preliminaries out of the way, I said, "I constructed an outline of the events on the boat so I can tell you what happened and when."

The tired detective looked at me. "Sure," he said. "Knock yourself out."

And so I told my story, referring to my timetable frequently. I kept my account as short as possible while making sure I covered everything I thought relevant. When I finished, I asked, "When will you know the results of the autopsies?"

Detective Gray asked a question instead of answering mine. "Why do you think Tiburon was strangled? Everyone else thinks he drowned."

"I work part-time as a forensic photographer for the Cliffview, California, police department," I said.

"So you've seen a lot of dead people, people who were strangled?"

"Well no. But I saw photos of them in my forensic photography course. Oh, I almost forgot. I photographed the body right after we recovered it from the sea."

"You took photos of the body?" The officer seemed dumfounded.

"Yes. I took full body shots, then close-ups of the head and neck. The ligature marks, the bruising and the discoloration of the face were all very evident."

Gray stared at me for several very long seconds before replying. "We're going to need those photos Ms Greene. Can you get them for me now?"

"The images are in my digital camera and that's in my room."

"I'll wait," Gray said.

When I opened the case in my room, though, the camera wasn't in its little foam nest. I dug through all of my luggage, carefully at first and then frantically, without success. Stuff was flung all over the room when I finally faced facts: The camera was gone.

The phone rang. "Are you coming back anytime soon?" Gray wanted to know.

"I can't find the camera," I said. "I don't remember what I did with it after I took the photos."

"Let's just finish the interview then," Gray suggested.

I slunk back to the interview room in a daze. I found it hard to focus on the questions; I was trying desperately to think what I'd done with that damn camera.

After I'd taken the photos, I'd gone into the galley with Kimberly. Had I set the camera down on the table there? I had no idea.

Detective Gray soldiered on, though he sometimes had to repeat a question before I heard him. At one point he asked, "By the way, did you mention your theory that Tiburon was strangled to anyone?"

"Only my boyfriend, Danny Decker. I just assumed Capt. Mac knew. He and his crew bagged the body. Surely they saw the marks on Tom's neck."

Gray's last question was: "Still no idea how Dave Pecot got in the freezer?"

"No," I said. "None at all."

Gray handed me his card. "If you think of anything or find that camera, give me a call."

I beat a hasty retreat.

Back in my room, I repacked all my stuff, hoping I'd missed the camera somehow. I hadn't. It simply wasn't there. I was getting ready for bed when someone knocked on the door.

It was a Miami PD officer with a search warrant. While waited outside in the hall, she went through my room and my luggage, confiscating and carting off everything that had a cord. After she left, I called Dad.

"Everyone's stuff has been searched," he said, "and no one knows why. It's really weird. They took small electrical appliances; the charger for Paul's electric shaver, Cathy's hairdryer and my battery chargers. Why on earth would they want those?"

I thought I knew. Still smarting from claiming to have photos and not being able to find them, however, I decided not to volunteer any more information. No point in making another statement I couldn't prove. Instead I said: "I told the officer who interviewed me about the photos I took of Tom's body. He wanted to see them but I can't find the little camera I used. Have you any idea what I did with it?"

"I remember you taking the pictures, honey. I knew I never should have suggested Chief Lawson hire you. When we get home, you need to tell him...."

"Dad. Did you see what I did with the camera?"

"No."

The officer who had searched my room left things in a mess. I repacked my luggage for the second time that day.

In bed later, I couldn't turn off my brain. The events I'd experienced kept running through it. Making matters worse, the room was way too cold with the air conditioner on but grew miserably hot when it was turned off. I developed a migraine. I stumbled to the bathroom shortly after 2:00 am and swallowed a couple of aspirins. Now I was thirsty. I pulled on a pair of shorts, found my purse and padded down the dimly lit hall to the vending machines. When the machine dispensed my Diet Coke, I headed back to my room.

That's when I noticed Mike. He was sitting on a chair in an alcove near the elevator, staring at the wall. He hadn't seen me. As I got closer, I saw tears glistening on the one cheek visible to me and could feel a sadness emanating from him. Although I wanted to comfort him, I didn't know how. Quiet as a mouse I returned to my room, closing the door softly behind me.

Chapter 14

A subdued group of divers assembled in the hotel lobby early the next morning. The search had kept all of us up late and been very distressing. It was all we talked about as we loaded our luggage onto the airport shuttle and climbed aboard.

Mike had Dave's stuff to schlep as well as his own and did it without complaining. He spoke only when he had to and then in monosyllables. The Mouse, however, was very vocal about the difficulties Tom's mountain of photo gear was causing her.

"I had to repack all of our stuff after that police officer went through it last night. I only got about two hours' sleep," she whined, "I just can't deal with this." Paul volunteered to take charge of one of Tom's suitcases while Pete hefted the dead photographer's bulging carry-on.

When I got on the bus, Danny was already sitting with Mike. He did not look at me as I went by. Since The Mouse was alone, I slipped in next to her.

"What did they take from your luggage?" I asked.

"My hair dryer," she said. "They took Tom's laptop and all his charger thingies, even the one for his electric shaver. I asked when I'd get them back and they said 'when the investigation is complete.' What are they investigating? Tom's and Dave's deaths were accidents."

Luckily, she didn't wait for an answer. She continued to complain for the rest of what turned out to be a mercifully short trip. After the first few minutes, I tuned her out, going over the recovery of Tom's body and my taking photos of it again and again in my mind. It was no use, I could not remember where I'd put the camera. It seemed to have disappeared into thin air.

Once we had checked our luggage and made it through security at the airport, the group scattered. Camaraderie was a thing of the past. We had had, it seemed, quite enough of each other. Kimberly (I decided I'd better start thinking of her with her real name so I didn't slip and call her The Mouse) and Cathy wandered off in opposite directions; Pete and Jessica settled down for breakfast in the busy food court and one by one the others simply disappeared down one corridor or another or into one of the many shops.

I bought a raisin bagel with cream cheese and a large coffee, found a relatively quiet seat at the gate, and got out my still unfinished Laura Lippman book.

Our flight to LAX departed on time. I'd hoped Danny would be my seatmate; instead I got stuck in the middle, between two strangers.

I spent the flight making myself crazy. I really loved Danny and this was the first major glitch in our relationship. I didn't understand why he'd gotten so upset when I told him Tom and Dave had been murdered. It was pretty obvious to me that their deaths weren't accidents. We'd had disagreements in the past and they hadn't led to his avoiding me. Why was he doing that now?

Our plane arrived in Los Angeles a few minutes early. We loaded our gear onto another shuttle bus and left the airport at dusk. While most of us slept on this last leg of the journey, I don't think Mike did. When I passed him on my way to the restroom halfway to Cliffview he was awake and staring out the window.

The shuttle let us off at Danny's dive shop, where we were met by a small tornado in the form of his eight-year-old son, Sam. He'd spent the week in San Francisco with his mother, Danny's ex-wife, and her second husband. Expecting twins, she was confined to bed until they were born and Sam was temporarily living with Danny. He'd go back to living with his mom and visiting Danny when the babies arrived.

Sam's a cool little kid and I really like him. Tonight, however, the way he prattled on and on about his visit with his mom was irritating.

"Dad! You should see mom. She's big as a VW Beetle. When you put your hand on her stomach you can feel the babies kick. Her neighbors have a boy my age. I got to go the zoo. Our rabbit at school died. Did you miss me? I missed you."

The shuttle's passengers got into cars and vanished into the night. In a few minutes, everyone was gone. Danny checked the bus

---

before it departed, making sure no one had left anything behind. It was a good thing he did because Tom's heavy carry-on was still in the overhead rack and one of his suitcases was in the pile with Danny's and mine.

"I'll take those to Kimberly," I offered. "I want to see how she's doing anyway."

"You're not interested in her welfare, you just want to pry into her life," Danny said. Those were the first words he had spoken to me in more than 24 hours and they bristled with hostility. Nonetheless, he gave me the landline number he had for the Tiburons.

Danny's part-time employee, Greg Tauchen, had been helping us with the luggage. "What happened on that trip?" he asked. "You were kinda vague when you called from Miami."

"It's a long story," Danny said, "And we're tired." He looked at his watch. "We've been up since 2:00 am local time. I'll tell you all about it tomorrow."

Danny and Sam dropped me at my place, lugging my bags upstairs and putting Tom's two pieces into my truck in the subterranean garage. Sam's constant chatter disguised the fact that Danny and I didn't talk at all. Before they left, Sam hugged me, than raced down the stairs. Danny was already halfway down. He'd left without saying good-bye. I stood in the open doorway, watching as Sam caught up with his dad and grabbed his hand. I didn't close the door until they were out of sight.

The air in my condo was as stale and silent as a tomb. I was exhausted. I'd survived a near hurricane, the murders of two fellow travelers and rejection by the man I loved. If I'd had the energy I would've cried.

Chapter 15

I called Kimberly when I got into work the next morning and told her about Tom's luggage; she suggested I bring it by about 6:00 and stay for dinner. Danny and Sam were invited, too, she said.

Danny wasn't thrilled to hear from me. He was busy that evening he said, teaching a scuba class. He'd gotten Sam a sitter.

"It's that cute 14 year old from next door, isn't it?" I asked. "Sam's heart will be broken when she starts dating and doesn't have time for him anymore."

"He might as well get used to the ways of women now," Danny said, "then it won't come as such a shock when he's older." He hung up before I could ask him what he meant.

Jet lag caught up with Dad and me long before the day was over. He went home after lunch; I left shortly thereafter. We'd been too busy to talk so he didn't know my theory that whoever murdered Tom had also killed Dave. He didn't even know there had been any murders.

At home, I took a nap, unpacked, did some laundry and paid bills that had arrived while I was gone. By the time I'd done all that, it was time to visit Kimberly.

The Tiburons lived in the tiny, extraordinarily affluent community of Beachland, a few miles north of Cliffview. Kimberly had provided directions and I got there without a hitch.

When I stopped in front of a sprawling estate surrounded by a ten foot tall, wrought iron fence, I was convinced I'd gotten the address wrong. I checked, then rechecked my notes. This was it all right. I just wasn't expecting anything this big. I couldn't see much of the mansion, it was at the end of a gently curving drive, shaded and shielded by trees.

The gate was closed but there was an intercom. I pressed the button and spoke my name when prompted by a voice on the other end.

The gates rolled open and I drove toward an enormous two-story Mediterranean style villa with cream-colored stucco and a red tile roof.

Property in Beachland is very pricey; this one had to be worth several million dollars.

I parked behind the Lincoln Navigator in the circular driveway and wrestled Tom's luggage out of my van. Luckily, both pieces had wheels. I pulled them to the front door and rang the bell.

A maid in a black and white uniform answered my ring. After the two of us got the luggage into the foyer, she showed me into a spacious room filled with antique furniture. Kimberly appeared before I had much time to look around.

She gave me a hug, smelling of a fabulous perfume I know only from the free samples given away in department stores.

"How are you?" I asked. She was dressed in jeans and a pale blue cashmere sweater. Her long blond hair was tied back with a blue ribbon and there was a blue silk scarf with a seahorse print around her neck. She looked tired.

"Oh, I'm okay, I guess. Rattling around in this huge old thing."

"It's quite impressive," I said. "I didn't know underwater photography paid so well."

"It doesn't," she said. "Tom inherited it from his father."

"What did his dad do?"

"He was Jefferson S. Tiburon, 'Lawyer to the stars.' Tom was his only child, from wife number one," Kimberly said.

"There were other wives?"

"He was divorcing number three so he could marry number four when he died," she said.

"Are you going to keep the house?"

"Heavens no. It's way too big and it's creepy at night. Want a tour?"

Kimberly became a little more animated as she showed me around the villa. I thought Jefferson Tiburon's study on the first floor particularly interesting. It appeared to be a kind of a shrine to its former occupant.

"Tom must have been very fond of his father," I remarked, looking at walls full of photos of the senior Tiburon with the rich and famous.

"He didn't really know him," Kimberly said. "Tom's parents divorced when he was a baby and he rarely saw his dad. But Tom was proud of him. That's why he became a lawyer. Got his degree at UCLA just like his dad."

"Tom had a law degree?" I was surprised. "I thought he'd majored in photography at Windgate."

"His father insisted he learn a practical vocation so Tom got his law degree first. He attended Windgate Institute of Photography later."

She didn't say, "After his father died and he inherited a lot of money," but she telegraphed that thought just as surely as if she'd spoken it out loud.

Something niggled my brain. "Mike Keating and Dave Pecot went to UCLA," I remembered, "and Mike is a lawyer. Did Tom know them before our trip?"

Kimberly frowned. "If he did he never mentioned it."

The villa and everything in it was in perfect condition. The wooden floors gleamed, the area rugs were freshly vacuumed and the air in all of the rooms smelled fresh. I figured Kimberly would need a good-sized staff to do all that work.

She took me through so many bedrooms and bathrooms that I lost count. She saved Tom's office on the second floor — right above his father's study — for last. It was a corner room. One set of windows offered a magnificent view of the Pacific, the other overlooked a beautiful swimming pool, two sets of tennis courts and a one-hole golf course.

While the rest of the house was a museum of fine furnishings from past eras, Tom's office was a modern photographer's dream. An impressive array of top of the line computers and a couple of high-end color printers sat on a desktop that ran along one wall. Shelves enclosed by glass doors held digital cameras, strobes, lenses and underwater housings.

The slides Tom had taken before the digital revolution were kept in climate-controlled cases. A ten-foot long light table had been custom built to view them.

One entire wall was taken up by a floor to ceiling bookcase containing an awesome collection of marine life references as well as what looked like every book on diving and underwater photography ever printed.

"Most photographers would give their right arms for this room,"

I said, browsing the bookshelves.

Then I saw the yearbook, lying on the floor at the base of the bookcase. I leaned down and picked it up.

"Oh," Kimberly said. "Tom must have gotten that out just before the trip."

The book was entitled, *Santa Barbara High 1990*. I opened it, thumbing through the pages idly.

"Didn't Tom go to private schools?" I asked.

Kimberly shrugged. "No. His mom didn't want him to grow up a rich kid brat. She sent him to public schools."

"She's still alive?"

"Died three years ago."

I was flipping through the pages of the yearbook when I saw the photo. It was labeled, "Most Devoted Couple." Tom hadn't changed much but at first I didn't recognize the girl standing next to him, she had yet to reach her full height. When I realized who she was, I was stunned.

"Tom and Jessica Wheeler were an item in high school," I said. "Did you know that?"

Kimberly looked annoyed. "He told me they went to school together, he didn't say they dated," she said. She took the yearbook and scrutinized the photo, then snapped it closed and dropped it on Tom's desk.

She glanced at her diamond-studded watch. "We should go downstairs," she said. "Cook gets upset if she has to hold dinner."

We ate in the huge dining room, served by an attentive waiter. The wine he poured had a name I recognized, though it's not one Danny and I can afford to order.

"I'm glad you could come," Kimberly told me as we munched on spinach salad with bacon dressing. "Meals here by all myself are dreadful."

"If you sell this place, where will you go?" I asked.

"Back to Santa Monica."

"Is that where you grew up?"

"Yes. That's where my family is."

"How long were you and Tom married?"

"Three years. We met at the opening of one of his photo shows in a Beverly Hills gallery."

A thought struck me. "Tom had lots of money, why didn't he hire a boat in the Bahamas? Heck, he could afford to buy one. Why go on a charter with other people?"

Kimberly sighed. "Tom used to own a boat. He had trouble keeping a crew because he was so abusive.

"He has chartered boats in the past. However, since he refused to pay for his last Bahamas trip, claiming the captain was incompetent, none of the dive boat owners in Miami or the Bahamas will even talk to him.

"When Tom heard about the last-minute opening on your trip, he jumped on it, figuring Capt. Mac wouldn't know he was coming till he got there."

Our entree was grilled salmon with a delicate mustard-white wine sauce. We also had fresh green beans and wild rice. There was raspberry sorbet for dessert. I cleaned my plate while Kimberly merely picked at her food.

"I thought the meals on the *DD II* were good but this was wonderful," I said. "If I cooked I'd beg for the recipes."

"I'll tell the staff," Kimberly said. "Maybe that'll make them happy. I don't have much of an appetite these days."

"Are you going to have a funeral for Tom?" I asked.

"There's going to be a small memorial service for family and staff," Kimberly said. "It would mean a lot to me if you and Danny came. It'll be here, at 3:00 next Wednesday."

Kimberly clung to me when I hugged her good-bye.

"See you next week," she said.

Chapter 16

Transiting from Highway 101 to the Cliffview off ramp, I made a spur of the moment decision, turning east toward Danny's place instead of west, toward mine.

Sam answered the door, accompanied by Sara, his cute babysitter.

"Cinnamon," he said, his initial delight at seeing me tempered by the fact that if I were there, Sara could go home. "Dad's not here. He has a scuba class tonight. Do you want to come back later?"

He looked so hopeful when he uttered that last sentence I didn't have the heart to disappoint him.

"Just tell him I dropped by," I said.

At my condo, I immersed myself in a raspberry scented bubble bath. Afterward, warm and drowsy, I got into bed and opened an S.J. Rozan book. I'd finished the Lippman on the flight home. I don't know how I fell asleep; I only meant to close my eyes for a few minutes.

Dad woke me early the next morning. "Have you had breakfast?" he asked over the phone. "The coffee's on and Sandy's making her special French toast. Smells pretty good in here right now."

Fortunately, or unfortunately, I'm not one of those people who needs to be persuaded to eat a home cooked meal. "I'll be right over," I said.

I washed my face and combed my hair, then pulled on jeans and a T-shirt before jogging to Sandy and Dad's. The house I grew up in burned to the ground just before they married and they'd built a new one on the lot. It was a magnificent Victorian reproduction with five bedrooms and three baths. At present, it was sparsely furnished; Sandy was looking for just the right antiques. The nursery, however, was ready, though the baby wasn't due for months.

A white picket fence surrounded the yard of the white-with blue-gingerbread trim house. In a nod to low maintenance, the fence was vinyl.

The front door wasn't locked and I let myself in. The aroma of freshly brewed coffee greeted me.

"We're in the kitchen, Cinnamon," Sandy yelled. She and Dad were sitting at the round oak table. Sandy wore a pale blue terrycloth bathrobe; Dad was dressed in khakis and a red polo shirt with the Greene's One Stop Camera Shop logo. He was mopping up the small puddle of syrup on his plate with a forkful of French toast.

I drank a glass of orange juice while Sandy fried two slices of bread for me.

She wasted no time with pleasantries. "You and Danny patched things up yet?" she asked.

"No," I said.

"Didn't think so," Dad said. "You didn't sit together on the trip home."

"You really don't know what's wrong?" Sandy asked, expertly flipping the bread slices.

"You're not going to give up, are you?" I asked.

"Nope," Sandy said. "We care too much about both of you to see you like this. You're miserable apart."

"I'm miserable," I said. "I wouldn't know about Danny."

"Trust me," Sandy said, slipping two pieces of French toast onto a plate, "Danny's miserable, too."

I slathered no-bad-stuff margarine on my toast and covered it with maple syrup.

"I think Danny's upset because I told him two people were murdered on our trip," I explained.

Dad looked at Sandy, Sandy looked at Dad, and then they both looked at me.

"Murdered?" they said in unison.

"Tom and Dave were murdered?" Dad sounded skeptical.

Still holding the pancake turner, Sandy sat down next to me. "Tom drowned during a night dive," she said. "And no one knows how Dave ended up in the freezer."

"Tom's gear wasn't used that night," I said. "His tank was full when we checked it the next morning. I think someone strangled him as he was getting ready to make the dive and pushed his body overboard. There were ligature marks on his neck."

"I saw a red line on his neck," Dad said. "But you can't possibly know when it happened. Maybe the body got wrapped in fishing line underwater."

"The mark was made before he died," I said. I cut a piece of toast with my fork and popped it into my mouth, enjoying the sweet taste. "Mind if I eat before discussing this further?"

"Please," Dad said.

"Delicious, as usual, Sandy," I said.

"Thanks," she said.

The two of them sat there, waiting impatiently for me to finish my toast and coffee. As Sandy poured me a second cup I said: "Chief Lawson loaned me several forensic books. I'd finished the section on strangulation in one of them before our trip. It causes a purple discoloration of the face and neck. Also, a ligature causes bruising only if it's applied when the victim is alive.

"Since the police confiscated our battery chargers, hair dryers and shavers, I'd guess they think Tom was strangled with an electrical cord."

"If you're right," Dad said, "who do you think killed Tom?"

I listed my suspects.

When I finished, Sandy shuddered. "I'm glad I didn't know there were murders on that little boat," she said. "I wouldn't have felt safe."

Dad asked, "What does Danny think?"

"That both of them were accidents," I replied. "He booked the charter and was the leader of our trip. I know he feels responsible for the safety of the group members. An accidental death would be bad enough, he doesn't want to believe there was one murder, let alone two."

Dad and Sandy were quiet for a while, thinking about what I'd said. Then Sandy asked: "You saw Kimberly yesterday. How is she?"

"She's not exactly the poor grieving widow," I said, describing the villa and the highlights of my visit. Then I remembered something. "Tom went to Santa Barbara High School," I said. "He and Jessica Wheeler were voted 'Most Devoted Couple' in their sophomore class. Did you know they knew each other before the trip?"

Both Sandy and Dad shook their heads "No."

"That's a surprise," Sandy said. "It's hard to imagine they ever had anything in common."

"Here's something else," I said. "Tom and Mike went to UCLA law school. Dave was a UCLA graduate as well.

"UCLA is huge," Dad pointed out. "They could all have been there at the same time and never met."

"I'd like to talk to Jessica," I said. "Maybe she's not the only one on our trip with a past linked to Tom's."

Chapter 17

Though tourists (they love our beaches) are mostly gone in Cliffview after the Avocado Festival in October, Greene's remained busy. Dad and I had missed an entire week of work and things had piled up. While the images I'd taken on the Bahamas trip had been downloaded to my laptop during the trip I hadn't had time to do a final edit. I also hadn't had time to call Jessica.

I hustled down to The Bakery just before noon and bought a sandwich, which I ate at my desk while answering e-mails. Greene's can't compete with online companies on the price of photo equipment and accessories so we go overboard on service. Our camera club offers trips with local experts to photograph birds, whales, monarch butterflies, harbor seals and wild flowers as well as Spanish missions and other nearby wonders; we sponsor and administer an e-list where people can post questions and "talk" to each other; and have a website where appointments can be made for portrait sittings and coverage of special events by still or video photography or both.

While Dad and I were gone, Miguel Takamura had gotten stuck with my tasks plus his own and there was a backlog. Now he was taking a few days off and I was doing two jobs. I spent most of the day on the internet, answering technical questions and working on the portrait and event calendars.

It was an incredible relief to open and answer the last e-mail. Before another could pop up on my screen, I logged off and put my computer to sleep. It was a half hour before closing. Rather than get involved in another project, I called Jessica.

"Come on over," she said. "We can talk while I prepare for my classes tomorrow."

I drove to her preschool in my "new" pick-up. It used to be

Dad's. He gave it to me for my birthday because he'd bought himself an SUV, which he considers more suitable for his growing family. I'm not complaining. A three-year-old truck is a considerable step up from my previous vehicle, a much abused eight-year-old van. I delight in all the amenities my new ride offers, especially the GPS. Since I got it I hardly ever get lost topside. The new truck will go 75 mph without complaining and only has 50,000 miles on it.

The school at which Jessica teaches is a couple of miles from Greene's. Cliffview, however, is so small everything is only a couple of miles away from everything else. I parked at the curb and went looking for Jessica.

She was sitting at her desk, tracing animal patterns onto construction paper. "We're getting ready for a trip to the zoo," she told me. "The children will color these. You can help if you like." The two of us traced several animals while we talked.

She was working on a lion when I mentioned Dave. "What a tragedy. He was really nice," she said. "I feel sorry for his family."

"Me, too," I said. "Jessica, I need to ask you something."

She finished the lion and started tracing a giraffe on yellow paper. "Ask away."

"Kimberly left two pieces of Tom's luggage on the shuttle," I said. "I took them to her last night. In Tom's study I picked up a Santa Barbara High School yearbook...."

Jessica interrupted. "You saw a photo of Tom and me. 'Most Devoted Couple.'" She put down her pencil. "I never would have signed up for the trip if I'd known he was going. When I saw him drive up that morning I almost got off the bus. Pete convinced me to stay.

"While Kimberly was in the restroom, Tom came over and asked me to pretend we didn't know each other," she continued. "He said his wife would be upset if she found out we'd dated.

"That suited me just fine. He was such a jerk."

"How long did you go together and what happened?" I asked. "If you don't mind telling me, that is." I chose a giant panda pattern and began tracing it on white paper.

"We had a few classes together in the beginning of our sophomore year. We were both skinny, socially inept nerds. He asked me to go to a dance with him and we began dating after that. I liked him but neither of us ever pretended it was love. It was convenient and comfortable.

"At the end of our junior year, Tom went to Europe with his mother. They spent the entire summer there. He sent post cards from all the places they visited and wrote me long letters.

"When he returned, we went out just once. Then he dumped me. He wouldn't tell me why. I was devastated."

Jessica carefully traced an eagle on dark brown paper. "It wasn't until I came across that yearbook picture years later that I figured out what I did wrong."

"What?" I asked.

"I grew." Jessica traced a tiger on orange paper. "When we started dating, Tom and I were the same height. By the end of our junior year, I was three inches taller. By the time he got back from Europe that summer, I was six inches taller. While it wasn't a big deal to me, I'm sure it was to him. He was quite sensitive about his height."

"Did you know his parents?" I asked, picking up an elephant pattern.

"We saw quite a lot of his mom, Martha. She was always very nice to me. Tom's love of the ocean came from her, she began scuba diving as a teenager.

"I only met Tom's dad once. We had dinner with him and wife number two at the mansion. Did you get to see much of it when you visited Kimberly last night?"

"She gave me an extensive tour," I said. "The house is fantastic."

Jessica continued. "Tom's dad, Jefferson, was generous with his money but not with his time. He died not long after Tom graduated from UCLA." She finished the tiger and selected a bear pattern.

"Did Tom's mother remarry?" I chose gray construction paper and traced an elephant.

"Nope. She got a nice financial settlement in the divorce. She opened an aquarium store here in town when Tom was in high school." Jessica finished the tiger.

"I remember that shop," I said. "It was in the strip mall near the beach. I went in there many times to look at the fishes. I remember the owner but I don't think her last name was Tiburon."

"Martha used her maiden name, Martin, after the divorce. She died about three years ago."

I set the elephant aside. "So both of Tom's parents are gone," I said.

Jessica nodded. "Jefferson was a heavy drinker and smoker. It was no surprise when he had a massive heart attack and died in his early 50s. You could see that coming. I was shocked to hear about Martha. She was bitten by the blue ringed octopus in one of her tanks just before Tom and Kimberly got married. The scuttlebutt was that it was suicide."

"Why would anyone think that?" I asked, choosing a camel and tan construction paper.

"It was a pet," Jessica said, "a tiny pet, only six inches long, tentacle to tentacle. She kept it in a special tank and enjoyed telling people how dangerous it was and how just one bite could kill a human. Then she'd put her bare hand into the water and feed it a piece of squid to show how docile it was.

"She was always careful. She never tried to pick the creature up. Yet she was found with the octopus in her fist."

"Any reason why she would self-destruct?" I asked.

"None that anyone could think of," Jessica answered. "She had no health or money problems and everybody liked her. The police insisted her death was an accident."

We were both silent for a few minutes, thinking our own private thoughts, then I asked: "Did anyone else know Tom before our trip?"

"Mike and Dave. They all went to UCLA," Jessica said.

"How do you know?" I asked.

"One night several of us were having cocktails on the sundeck. We were complaining about Tom, as usual," Jess said. "I said Tom had been a world class jerk in high school. Mike said he and Dave had had quite enough of Tom in college. They almost got off the bus when they saw him get on."

Chapter 18

Danny called in early evening. Instead of every day, I'd seen him only a couple times since we'd gotten home and on each occasion he'd been distant. The one time we'd gone out to dinner, he had invited another couple so there was no chance for meaningful discussion. The one night we'd spent together the contact had produced the desired physical result but the emotional connection was definitely missing. Afterward, he rolled over and went to sleep.

The crush of work was a distraction and helped filled the void, but I missed the old Danny, the one I'd known before our trip. When things slowed down at Greene's, I had to figure out a way to make things right between us.

On the phone now, Danny wanted to know if I was going diving that week. We were both members of the Wednesday Warriors, a group that chartered Santa Barbara's *California Diver* one Wednesday every month. I said I couldn't; I'd told Kimberly I'd attend Tom's memorial service.

"Do you want to go with me?" I asked.

"Absolutely not," Danny said. "It would be hypocritical. I didn't like the man when he was alive, I don't like him any better now that he's dead. Besides, we're going to dive Capt. Steve's secret lobster spot off Santa Cruz. We did quite well there last year."

"I'd love to go. If I hadn't promised The Mouse I would."

"Have fun," Danny said. There wasn't a shred of sympathy in his voice.

It was a strange group that gathered at the Tiburon residence on the appointed afternoon. There were 12 of us, including Tom's aunt and her two sons; both Tom's lawyer and his accountant; and the villa's staff; three women and two men. I overhead the aunt asking

Kimberly why Tom's grandparents weren't there but didn't hear her answer. Everyone looked uncomfortable. No one looked sad.

We stood stiffly in the living room, munching on hors d'oeuvres served by a caterer so the villa's staff could attend the ceremony. After awhile, Kimberly asked us to go out on the large patio overlooking a steeply sloping hillside and the Pacific Ocean. It was a beautiful sunny day with a slight breeze.

Kimberly conducted the ceremony herself, reading several long passages from an Eastern philosophy book I'd never heard of.

My attention wandered. I surreptitiously observed the people around me. When Kimberly finished reading and started talking about how much she missed Tom, their expressions ranged from disbelief to boredom. Only one person, the aunt, displayed grief, weeping noisily. Eventually, one of her sons told her, a little too loudly I thought, "Get a grip, Mother."

When she finished, Kimberly handed a silver urn to one of the mansion's staff members saying, "Would you scatter the ashes, John?"

John took the top off the urn and removed a white bag. As he upended the bag over the low stone wall at the edge of the patio, the ashes were caught on the breeze and began swirling around and among the onlookers.

There was a collective gasp of horror, followed by exclamations of dismay. I turned my back to the wind, covering my eyes and mouth with my hands.

Kimberly was furious. "You idiot. Can't you do anything right? You've ruined everything."

That sounded most un-Mouse like. When I looked at her, her face was twisted in fury.

John turned white. He set the urn on the edge of the wall and, like everyone else, began brushing ashes out of his hair and off his clothing. It was a most unpleasant task.

"That's it," Kimberly said. "I've had enough of your incompetence. You're fired, John."

"Thank God," John said. "Out of my misery at last."

Kimberly confronted the rest of us. "It's over," she said. "Go home." She stalked into the house, leaving us standing there. The staff dispersed quickly and the lawyer seemed to disappear into thin air. Tom's aunt approached me and extended her hand.

"Thank you for coming," she said. "I'm sure Tom appreciated

it."

"He's dead, Mom," one of her sons said. "He can't appreciate anything. Not that he appreciated anything when he was alive."

"I know, dear," she said. "But he was so cute when he was little."

She and the two cousins walked into the house, leaving me alone on the patio with the urn. I folded the white bag, stashed it inside the box-like urn and closed the lid. Then I carried the urn into the living room and set it on the fireplace mantle, which seemed the most appropriate place.

The house was quiet when I let myself out the front door. I drove home thinking about the bizarre scene I'd just witnessed.

When I got to Greene's, I told Dad about the service. He thought it was funny.

"I believe there's a piece of Tom on the top of your head," he said.

I shuddered and ruffled my hair with both hands. "Guess you had to be there," I told him. "It was no laughing matter."

I had only been in the store for an hour when Danny called from the *California Diver*. He sounded like his old self, there wasn't a trace of coldness in his voice. Although I was a bit confused by the change I decided not to make an issue out of it. At least he was talking to me again. I could straighten things out between us later.

"Cinnamon," he said. "We had a great day. I got two lobsters. One's an eight pounder. But I don't want to cook tonight so Pete, Jess, Sam and I are having dinner at Juanita's at 6:30. Want to join us?"

"Sure," I said. "I'll meet you there."

When Greene's closed I went home and took a shower, then dressed in jeans and a T-shirt. I packed a small bag with clothes and stuff for tomorrow in case Danny wanted me to spend the night. I would leave the bag in the car and retrieve it if necessary.

Pete and Jessica were already at Juanita's when I arrived. Danny and Sam arrived a few minutes later. Their hair was still damp and they smelled of Danny's favorite soap.

When we were seated and the adults were enjoying ice cold Carte Blancas, along with tortilla chips and guacamole, Jessica asked me about Tom's memorial service. When I finished relating what had happened, she remarked, "It's odd that his mother's parents weren't there. They live in Santa Barbara. Tom was their only grandkid and they adored him."

"Maybe they're in poor health," I said. "They must be pretty old."

Jess thought a moment. "They're 83. I saw an article in the newspaper about a seniors' walking group last year. It said Ginnie and George Martin were its oldest members. They were still active then."

"Maybe they don't like Tom's little gold digger of a wife," Pete said.

"Kimberly?" I asked, astonished.

"It had to be the money, why else would she put up with Tom?" Pete asked. "And they were more alike than you'd think. That helpless kitten act is just that, an act."

"That would be my guess," Danny said.

I sat there with my mouth open. "I don't believe it," I said.

"You weren't in the stateroom next to them," Jessica said. "Kimberly played The Mouse in public but when they were alone, she and Tom would go at it like you wouldn't believe."

"Man, could she scream," Pete added.

"I still can't believe it," I said, but then the memory of Kimberly's face, twisted with rage over the urn incident, popped into my head.

Sitting next to Danny, Sam had been listening. "What's a gold digger?" he asked.

"Someone who marries someone else for their money," Danny said. "It's not something I'll ever have to worry about. Although if lobsters were worth their weight in gold I'd be doing okay."

The talk then shifted to the day's diving and the lobsters Pete and Danny had caught and almost caught. Tom and Kimberly were forgotten.

As we were leaving the restaurant, it wasn't Danny but Sam who asked, "Cinnamon. Are you coming over? I got stuff to show you."

I gave Danny time to tell him tonight wasn't a good night for that but he didn't.

I spent some time with Sam in his room, admiring a new poster of his favorite teen idol, a test he'd aced and few other things. I thought I'd get to talk to Danny once Sam went to bed but that didn't happen. A successful day of lobster hunting is an aphrodisiac for Danny. Our lovemaking was intense and immensely satisfying. I drifted off to sleep with a contented smile on my face.

Chapter 19

A good night's sleep was not in the books for me. My cell phone rang about 2:00 am. It was the Chief of Police, John Lawson.

He recited an address, told me it was a domestic abuse case and said I needed to go there right away.

Lawson is personally supervising my part-time job as forensic photographer. I think he's hoping I won't be up to the task and he'll be able to fire me. He hadn't wanted me for the job; he'd wanted Dad.

I stumbled out of bed and splashed water on my face, then threw on jeans and a sweater. The address was only a few minutes away.

The chief and I are not on the best of terms; we'd had some problems when I was in high school. There was that Lover's Lane incident, then the Halloween prank that nearly landed me in jail. While I thought he'd over-reacted on both occasions, the chief seemed to think I had the makings of a juvenile delinquent.

Lawson and Dad have been friends for decades. When Cliffview PD decided to go digital, Lawson sought Dad's advice and bought the equipment from Greene's.

The cop who set up the new system, however, quickly discovered there weren't all that many chances to use it. A few months later, he went to work for the Los Angeles County Sheriff's Department Crime Lab, where, Lawson predicted with a snort, "They'll work him till he drops."

Since no one else in the Cliffview PD knew how to use the digital equipment Lawson had just shelled out big bucks for, he offered the job to Dad. He pointed out it would only be a few hours a month. Dad declined, saying he'd be in the doghouse with Sandy if he took on another activity with a new baby on the way. He suggested me.

Lawson wasn't happy about that. He hired me only because he had no other candidates for the job.

I took it partly because I thought it would be interesting and I could use the extra money and partly because I knew it would irritate Lawson.

He loaned me a couple of books and I started reading up on the subject, which turned out to be fascinating. I was hooked long before I finished the first text.

Before tonight, I'd only had two calls: one had been a domestic abuse case, the other a fatal car crash. I'd taken to leaving Cliffview PD's cameras, a couple of lenses and two strobes locked in the pick-up's security box so I'd be ready at all times.

Tonight's address belonged to a well-kept unit in a small trailer park on the east side of Highway 101. It was easy to find because there were two police cars parked in front of it. The chief must have heard me pull up because he opened the door before I could knock. In his late 40s, Lawson was a trim and fit six-footer with cold, pale blue eyes. Before he opted to shave his head, he wore his blond hair clipped short.

Another officer was interviewing the victim, who looked to be in her late 30s. Her left eye was swollen shut, the right one was turning black and there were several big bruises on both of her upper arms.

She wept as she described how her husband had come home drunk after a night out with the boys and started a fight with her. She was three months pregnant and said she wanted to press charges this time because, "When it was just me it didn't matter that much but I can't let him hurt my baby."

While she was talking, there was a scuffle going on in another room. I gathered policemen there were trying to subdue the husband, who was shouting obscenities at them.

Not long afterward, they escorted him through the room we were in and out the door. The woman shrank back in her chair when she saw him and her husband threw her a menacing glance.

I wondered if she would manage to leave him and, if she did, if she'd ever feel safe.

When the interview was over, Lawson introduced me to the victim and asked me to photograph her injuries.

I was back at Danny's 45 minutes later. I fell into bed and a deep, dreamless sleep.

Danny and Sam were up early, as usual. I heard them leave the house. When they returned a short while later, I knew they'd been to The Bakery. In a few minutes, the smell of French roast coffee pulled me out of bed and into the kitchen.

"It's a beautiful morning, Sunshine," Sam said.

"Morning," Danny said. There was a chill in his voice. I looked up. His eyes weren't friendly and there was no smile on his face. He poured me a glass of orange juice and a cup of coffee. Sam set a gooey pecan bun on a plate in front of me. A newspaper was lying on the tabletop, so I picked it up.

The story on the front page was a shocker. "Crystal Family Mourns Tragic Death," the headline read. Under it were two photos, one of Dave Pecot, the other of Luke Crystal with his arm around a pretty, much younger blond.

Crystal, whose silver mane and chiseled profile made him instantly recognizable, was the charismatic pastor of Ventura's largest church. The congregation numbered in the thousands and had recently constructed a magnificent facility called Temple Crystal.

With a guilty start, I realized I'd gotten so involved in the affairs of Tom and Kimberly that I'd nearly forgotten Dave, the second victim on our trip.

I took a closer look at the picture of Luke Crystal and the blond. The caption said she was his daughter, Laura Pecot. Now I knew why the photo Dave had shown me on *Dolphin Diver II* had looked so familiar.

"Did you know Dave's wife was Luke Crystal's daughter?" I asked Danny.

"Not until I read that article," Danny said. "Dave told me he was married to a preacher's daughter and that he was the church's accountant. But he never mentioned the name of the church or his father-in-law."

"Maybe he didn't talk about him on purpose," I said. "Crystal's ultra conservative views aren't popular with all segments of the community."

I picked up the paper and continued reading, this time out loud.

"David Irwin Pecot, Temple Crystal's head accountant and husband of Luke Crystal's only child, Laura, died unexpectedly during a scuba diving vacation in the Bahamas," the article said. "When the ship docked in Miami, Pecot's body was discovered in the ship's walk-in freezer, near the body of another passenger who died earlier on the trip. Pecot died of hypothermia. Toxicology tests are pending.

"The circumstances surrounding the death of the other passenger, well known underwater photographer Tom Tiburon of Beachland, are also bizarre. He never returned from a night dive and his body was recovered from the ocean two days later.

"Police say Tiburon was murdered but haven't released any details about the crime.

"While Pecot and Tiburon were both UCLA graduates, they were not close friends. The police won't confirm that their deaths are related."

I looked at Danny when I finished that last paragraph, wanting to gauge his reaction. But he had turned his back on me and begun washing the breakfast dishes. There was no point in talking to him with the water running, so I finishing reading the article to myself. There were no more bombshells, only information I already knew.

A few minutes later, Danny asked, "What kind of case did you have last night?"

"Domestic abuse," I said.

"Anyone I know?"

"You know I can't tell you that," I said.

"I don't know why you took that job. Photographing dead bodies and beat-up people, it's ghoulish. I don't like that you get calls in the middle of the night and I don't like that you have secrets."

"I've only gotten one call at night," I said. "As for secrets, you seem to have plenty of your own, Danny. We're way overdue for a...."

I had a lot more to say but Sam bounded into the room just then. It was time for school and work.

I figured I hadn't heard the end of one particular subject, though. I wondered if Danny was focusing on my new job to avoid talking about the real issues between us, whatever they were.

Chapter 20

It took a while, but we finally eliminated the work backlog. And today, business was light. That was fine with me. After lunch, I finally had time to look at the images from the Bahamas trip.

Several of the best were on my computer screen when Dad walked in.

"You did great, honey."

"Wish I had the photos I took of Tom's body. I still can't figure out what I did with that damn camera. It's driving me nuts. Kimberly grabbed me. I took her into the galley and sat her down. She was dripping wet so I wrapped towels around her. What did I do with the camera?"

"Obviously you put it down somewhere," Dad said. "And maybe somebody else moved it to a safer place. Who packed Tom's photo gear? Maybe it's in with his stuff."

That gave me hope. I phoned Kimberly, described the missing camera and asked if she would look through Tom's photo equipment for it.

"I don't know anything about Tom's photo gear, John was in charge of it," she said. "He unpacked it the day you brought it here and didn't mention finding anything that wasn't Tom's. If you like, however, you can check it out yourself."

We agreed I would come by the next afternoon. After we had hung up, I remembered Jessica's connection to Tom. Then I recalled that he, Dave and Mike had all gone to UCLA. I wondered what had happened there to make them enemies.

It wasn't until I was answering e-mails, however, that the idea came to me. As usual, there was lots of spam, including one from an internet site devoted to reuniting school classmates. I usually delete those immediately. I still live in the small town in which I grew up and know far more than I want to about my former classmates, courtesy of the local gossip mill.

But maybe that website would help me figure out the relationships among Tom, Dave and Mike. I directed my browser to the site. In order to access it I'd have to become a member. I filled out the form and payment info. I made myself a UCLA graduate the same year as Tom. I'm actually a Windgate Institute alumna, several years younger than he was. Not long afterward I was able to peruse the list of registered UCLA alumni from the time period I'd chosen.

Unfortunately, none of the three men appeared to be members of the site and I had no idea which of the people who were might know them. Besides, I had work to do. I logged off and went about Greene's business.

The next afternoon, I got to the Tiburon villa precisely on time. I was surprised to find the gate open. I drove in and parked in the circular driveway.

Kimberly answered the door, looking pale and wan.

"I'm so glad you're here," she said. "I'm going batty all alone."

"Where's your staff?" I asked.

Kimberly frowned. "They all quit yesterday," she said.

"What? Why?"

Kimberly shrugged. "I have no idea. One minute they were here, the next minute they were gone. Maybe they didn't like having a female boss.

"This house is so spooky at night. I closed the gate, turned on the alarm and locked myself in my bedroom but even so, I didn't sleep a wink.

"I just don't know how I'll manage. This is all so overwhelming."

Afraid tears might flow I tried to distract Kimberly. "Maybe we should look for my camera," I suggested.

Kimberly led me up the stairs and down the hall to her husband's office. Tom's photo cases had been neatly stowed in a closet built to accommodate them, probably by the now-departed John. I pulled out the huge one he'd had on the trip. It was empty. Kimberly pointed out another case Tom had taken on the trip. It, too, was empty.

"How about his suitcase?"

"The staff unpacked it," Kimberly said. "The cameras would have been put in here somewhere. Feel free to look."

The next half hour was spent searching the drawers, equipment cases, cupboards and closets in the office. Tom had been meticulous; as near as I could tell there was a place for everything and everything was in its place. While there were several point and shoot cameras, none was mine.

"I was so sure it would be here," I said, browsing the titles of the wonderful library that covered one wall. The tomes were catalogued and filed the way they would have been in a regular library. "Where did Tom get all these books? I've never heard of most of them."

"He had a local bookstore order every underwater book for him as soon as it was published," Kimberly told me. "A librarian came in to catalogue and shelve them several times a year. Tom was obsessive about having every book he owned in his database, even his school yearbooks."

"Really?" I said. "Now where would they be?"

Kimberly pointed to a section of the bookcase and there, shelved together by year, were the yearbooks from Tom's junior high, high school and colleges. I pulled out the one for his sophomore year at UCLA.

"Do you mind if I look at this?" I asked.

Kimberly shrugged. "Be my guest," she said.

I thumbed through the book, trying to look casual. The index in the back listed Tom's name and the three pages that contained pictures of him. One was of the university's dive club, the other, the fencing club. Dave Pecot and Mike Keating weren't in either photo.

The third picture was of a fraternity. I picked out Tom immediately and then Mike, who hadn't changed all that much. Standing next to him was Dave Pecot, nearly unrecognizable with a full head of hair.

"Did you know Tom, Dave and Mike were in the same fraternity in college?" I asked.

"He may have mentioned that," Kimberly said. "I don't remember."

"Can I borrow this?" I asked.

"Take it," Kimberly said. "Just return it when you're finished. Do you have time for a cup of coffee?"

I checked my watch. "Sorry, I've got to run. I've got a portrait sitting in half an hour."

As I drove back to Greene's, I mulled over how deceptive

appearances can be. I considered myself an observant person yet I'd spent nearly a week with a small group of people, failing to realize that several of them had not only known but probably hated each other for a couple of decades.

When Danny called I told him about my trip to the mansion, explaining, "My little point and shoot camera is missing. I was hoping it had been put in Tom's luggage by mistake." I didn't mention I'd used that camera to take photos of Tom's body and what I really wanted were the images in it.

"E-mail Mac," Danny suggested. "Ask him if he found a camera on the boat." He gave me Mac's e-mail address, which I wrote down.

"It's worth a try," I said. "Oh, by the way, I have one of Tom's college yearbooks. He, Dave and Mike were in the same fraternity at UCLA. The plot thickens."

"There is no plot," Danny said.

And just like that, he was gone. Wow. A bit out of sorts, I carried the yearbook to Dad's office. I told him my camera hadn't been in Tom's stuff, then opened the book and showed him the photo of Tom, Mike and Dave together.

"That's a surprise," Dad said. "Those three didn't act like old acquaintances."

"No, they didn't," I agreed. "But neither did Jessica and Tom and they dated for nearly two years.

"By the way," I continued. "Danny doesn't like that I'm working for the Cliffview PD."

"Imagine that," Dad said. I'd get no sympathy from him.

I went back to my office and e-mailed Mac: "I can't find my point and shoot camera. Last time I saw it was in the galley. Did you find one?" I added the camera's make and model.

That night, as I lay alone in my bed in the dark, I reflected on my previously wonderful relationship with Danny. It was broken and I didn't know how to fix it.

Shortly after midnight I heard the wail of Cliffview's fire engines. I'll sort this out tomorrow, I told myself, and drifted off to sleep.

Chapter 21

The call came just before sunrise.

"Cinnamon? This is Tony d'Argent, Cliffview Police Department. I need you for a crime scene shoot ASAP."

I yawned. "Don't criminals ever work decent hours?" I asked.

D'Argent laughed. "Their inability to fit in is one of the reasons they turn to a life of crime," he said. "Pick you up in 15. I'll bring coffee."

I put on the first warm clothes I found, gray sweatpants and a matching sweatshirt, then rode the elevator to the subterranean garage to get Cliffview PD's camera bag out of my truck. I didn't notice the time but the sky was just beginning to lighten as I walked up the driveway to the sidewalk. A Cliffview PD patrol car was already waiting at the curb.

The driver rolled the window down, "Cinnamon?" he asked. I nodded, then walked over to the passenger door and got in.

The man handed me an extra large cup of coffee. "It's black," he said, "there's cream and sugar in the bag."

"Black is good," I replied.

As we drove to the scene in d'Argent's black and white I surreptitiously checked him out. I knew all of the Cliffview PD's officers by sight. Before today, however, Tony and I had never actually met, which, I decided, was too bad. He was very attractive, with a trim, solid body, olive skin and very dark brown eyes. His shiny black hair was clipped short and his upper lip was clean-shaven. He was exceptionally neat, exceptionally polite and exceptionally serious, not to mention exceptionally taciturn.

After a couple of sips of coffee I asked, "Where's the chief?"

"On vacation."

"Where are we going?"

"Possible arson."

"Those the sirens I heard last night?"

"Yes."

That was the extent of the conversation. Less than ten minutes after Tony picked me up, we were at the fire site, staked out with yellow crime scene tape.

The badly burned small, one story building bore a blackened sign in front that said it was an automobile upholstery shop. There was little left of the four-room structure but a charred skeleton and puddles of water. An acrid smell clung to the site.

"I've never done an arson before," I said.

"No problem. First we'll get overall photos of the building, then I'll go through it alone and make notes while you finish your coffee," Tony said.

We walked around the perimeter together, with him telling me what shots he wanted. When we finished, I sat in the car and watched him work. He moved quickly through what remained of the building, taking notes. He stopped every now and then to look at something more closely. I drained my cup long before he came back.

"Follow me and be careful where you step," he said. "Use my footprints whenever you can."

I did as directed. We started at the back. Tony's running commentary held my attention. First he pointed out that the back of the building was slightly less damaged than the front.

"Someone doused a couch in the front of the building with gasoline. Then they dribbled gasoline to the back door and torched the trail. The floor's wood and the fire spread quickly."

"How do you know the accelerant was gasoline?" I asked.

"You can smell it."

I sniffed the air. He was right.

"This was the container." Tony pointed to a melted red plastic blob. "We'll need wide angle shots that show exactly where it was found along with close-ups of it."

When I finished those, Tony used gloves to pick up the container and put it in a paper bag, which he labeled. Then he took me through the house, referring to his notes as he went. "Here's where they poured the gasoline," he said, pointing to a trail of charred wood.

I took photos of that and the various other things Tony requested. He collected a few more items and put them in paper bags. We headed toward the front of the building

"Notice that the couch is burned more than the area surrounding it?" he asked. "That's a sign an accelerant was used."

I took photos of the couch from several angles. I liked working with Tony. Chief Lawson hadn't ever been forthcoming about the reasons for taking photos and he definitely hadn't encouraged questions.

We worked steadily for quite awhile. Finally, Tony straightened up and looked around.

"Guess that's it," he said. "We're finished. Do you want to download the photos at the station now or later?"

"Later," I said. "I need to eat first."

"I'll treat you to breakfast at the station," Tony said. "The coffee's pretty good and there might even be a couple of doughnuts left."

"Great," I said. "I'm starved."

Tony smiled for the first time, revealing movie star perfect white teeth. "Nothing like a crime scene to build an appetite," he said.

A few minutes later, we were parking in the Cliffview PD lot.

"I didn't think I could function this early," I said. "Did I remember to comb my hair?" I ran my fingers through my short reddish-brown hair, noticing there were ashes on my clothes. Tony's uniform and shoes were still spotless.

"You look just fine," Tony said. His frank appraisal made me blush. I'd choose the outfit for my next crime scene shoot more carefully.

I brushed off ashes as we got out of the car and went into the station. Tony sent me down the hall to the break room, explaining he'd join me after the evidence bags were logged in. I chose a chocolate covered doughnut. Since I'd already had enough coffee, I plunked a few coins in a vending machine for a bottle of orange juice.

I ate the doughnut and sipped the juice while sitting at a round, faux wood topped table. Sunlight streamed through windows high on one wall. The room was a robin's egg blue, with a wood patterned vinyl floor. It was neat and clean.

Tony showed up a few minutes later. "How do you like forensic photography?" he asked, pouring a cup of coffee.

"I love it," I said. "It's so interesting. And I really enjoy working with you. The chief directs, he doesn't explain."

"You won't learn anything that way," Tony said. "The goal should be for you to photograph scenes on your own after talking to the cop who's investigating the fire."

"I'd like that," I said. "But I get the feeling Lawson hopes I'll quit. I wasn't his first choice, he wanted my dad."

Tony chuckled. "You're doing fine. He'll come around. But it might take awhile."

"How long have you been with the Cliffview PD?" I asked.

"Five years," Tony said. "I was with the San Diego PD for three years before that."

"You don't find it boring here?"

"Nope. I'm a small town guy."

"Your parents live nearby?"

"Ojai."

"Any siblings?"

"Two sisters. How about you?"

"I'm an only child at present," I said, "but Dad's new wife is pregnant."

"Ah yes, Sandy. So you're only now going to have a little brother or sister and you're how old?"

"Over 30," I said. "How old are you?"

"Under 30," Tony said. "But I like older women." He smiled again, showing those beautiful teeth.

That flustered me. With no snappy retort to cover my embarrassment, I washed down the last bite of doughnut with orange juice while avoiding Tony's intense brown eyes.

"Why the name Cinnamon?" Tony asked after a few minutes of silence.

"I was born with bright red hair. My mother said it was the color of cinnamon."

"You grew up here, didn't you?"

"Yes," I said. "After I got married, I lived in Hollywood for nearly a decade. I returned to Cliffview last year."

"I heard your husband is famous. What's his name?"

"Ted Quiero. He's a celebrity photographer. He's shot a couple of Rolling Stone covers. He's my ex-husband, though, we're divorced."

"Is he from Cliffview?"

"No, he was born and raised in LA. We met at Windgate

Institute." I was beginning to feel grilled and changed the subject. "How about you? You ever been married?"

"Still waiting for the right girl," Tony said and winked at me. I felt the color rise in my face and drank the rest of my juice in one gulp.

"Better download those photos. Thanks for breakfast." I stood up.

"Let me know when you're finished and I'll give you a lift to the camera store."

"Thanks, but I'd better walk," I said. "I need to work off that doughnut."

I thought he seemed disappointed.

Chapter 22

After downloading the arson photos, I walked to Greene's, only a couple of blocks away. I was a few minutes early; Dad wasn't even there yet. I went to my office, turned on the computer and checked my e-mail. I read Capt. Mac's message first.

"Hey Half-pint," he'd written. "Sorry, no extra cameras on the boat. One of my guests found something else, though. I sent it to you. You might get it today. "

He'd typed "Mac," under the last sentence then added: "P.S. "Two bottlenose dolphins, got to be the ones that brought Tom to us, hung around the boat for several days on our last trip. We think they're a pair of trained dolphins that escaped from the Oceanarium in Freeport a few months ago."

Trained dolphins. That explained a lot of things. I remembered the look on the police officer's face when I told him dolphins had brought Tom's body to us. He'd been incredulous. It was so bizarre I hardly believed it myself. In my mind's eye I saw the dolphin watching when I grabbed Tom's arm. It didn't leave till I'd said, "Thank you." Trained dolphins might do that. One mystery solved, two huge ones to go.

Since I had time, I opened Tom's yearbook to the page with the dive club photo. Someone in that photo must know why Tom, Mike and Dave disliked each other. While the names of the people were listed under the photo, tracking them down, especially since a couple of decades had passed, would be time consuming.

I logged onto the school reunion website I'd joined earlier. Then I examined the yearbook photo, listing the names of everyone in it on a piece of paper. Eventually I found three people on the alumni list who were also in the dive club photo. While I couldn't contact them directly, the site would forward an e-mail message to them. If they chose to, they could answer.

I thought for a while, trying to come up with some way to make the people want to e-mail me back. Finally I composed the following message: "I am writing a history of the UCLA diving club. May I interview you about your experiences as a member?"

I sent that message to the three club members who were on the alumni list, then turned to the yearbook page that had the fraternity photo that included Tom, Dave and Mike. That netted five more names on the alumni list. I sent those men the following message: "I am writing a history of your UCLA fraternity. Would love to interview you about your experiences as a member. Please contact me."

The package Mac had mentioned arrived late that afternoon. Inside it I was surprised and saddened to find Dave Pecot's logbook. The note with it read: "One of our passengers found this half-buried in the sand on the Sugar Wreck. We dried it out in the engine room. Maybe Dave's wife would like it. Mac."

After weeks on the bottom of the sea the logbook was badly damaged. The red cover had faded to pink and was marred by scratches. Though the writing on the pages was still legible, rust from the metal three-ring assembly had rubbed off on them.

I remembered finding the matching pen on the deck as we were leaving the *DD II*. I rooted around in my purse and found it, returning it to its rightful place in the logbook.

Then, feeling like a voyeur, I thumbed through the log. Mike had said reading it put him to sleep. It was easy to see why. Dave wrote in a minuscule script and he did, indeed, note everything he saw and at what depth he saw it. It was rather mind numbing. He also kept track of the usual things; visibility, maximum depth and time spent underwater. In the space allotted for "buddy" there was only one name throughout: Mike Keating.

The last entry in the log was dated the day before Tom went missing. Rather than describing an encounter with spotted dolphins, Dave had detailed the scars and distinguishing marks on the animals so he could recognize them if he saw them again.

Afterward, I took the logbook into Dad's office and explained how I'd gotten it.

"Shouldn't you send it to the Miami cops?"

"Can't think why they'd want it. It's just a list of what he saw underwater. A total snooze."

"Mike might appreciate that log more than Mrs. Pecot," Dad said. "He went on those trips with Dave."

"That's what I thought," I said. "But the widow will have to make that decision, not me."

Chapter 23

Before the Bahamas trip, Danny and I had had contact every day, even if only by e-mail. Now, three days passed without my hearing from him. Dozens of times I thought of things I wanted to tell him. I sent e-mails and phoned his shop and home, leaving voice messages. There was no response. I developed a dull ache in my chest in the vicinity of my heart. I lost my appetite. I longed to see him.

On the afternoon of the third day I dropped by Cliffview Divers. Greg Tauchen, Danny's part-time employee, told me his boss was running errands and wouldn't be back in the shop till the following day. I asked Greg if he knew what was wrong between Danny and me. Greg claimed not to know. I didn't believe him.

I was also frustrated by the lack of response from the eight e-mails to UCLA alumni. Only one person, a woman who'd been on the dive team, had e-mailed me back. She said she was traveling and wouldn't be able to do an interview until she got back to the U.S. She'd contact me then, she said. Yeah, right, I thought.

My life was unsettled and I was restless. I had trouble concentrating. When Tony called, requesting my presence at the scene of a crash, I welcomed the diversion.

The accident involved three cars on one of Cliffview's main streets. An SUV had run a red light and broadsided a compact sedan, which was rear-ended by a pick-up. Although all of the vehicles were severely damaged, none of the occupants was seriously injured.

The scene was chaotic. All of Cliffview's black and whites were there, along with two ambulances and a couple of fire trucks. The lookie-loos were out in force.

Once again, Tony was exceptionally professional, telling me exactly what he wanted me to do and why. I photographed all of the cars together, then separately, from several different angles. I shot the insides of each vehicle and photographed the tire treads.

When we'd finished and I was heading to my truck, Tony caught up to me.

"Cinnamon," he said, "I've got a job for you. If you're available, that is."

I turned, realizing for the first time that he wasn't as tall as I'd thought; he was a couple of inches under six feet. Also for the first time, he seemed ill at ease. When he spoke, the words came out in a rush. "We're celebrating my mother's 50th birthday this weekend and would like you to photograph the party. Can you do it?" He studied my face with those very intense brown eyes. He was so close I could smell the faint scent of his aftershave.

Tony frowned, then added, "Sorry to be asking so late, my family's a little disorganized and we only just thought of this."

"I'd be happy to do it," I told him, "But I'm booked Saturday."

"The party is Sunday," Tony brightened. "Are you free that day?"

"I am. Just tell me where and when."

"The Golden Oak Spa and Resort in Ojai. The party starts at 3:00. Come a little early."

"That's a beautiful setting for a party. Your mother's a lucky woman," I said.

"See you there then," Tony said, smiling.

He remained at the accident scene while I went to the station to download the photos. I stopped at Cliffview Divers before heading back to Greene's.

Once again, Danny wasn't there. Greg said the compressor was down and Danny had gone to Ventura to get a part for it.

"Why is he avoiding me?" I asked. "I'm not leaving till you tell me."

"He hasn't confided in me," Greg said, reluctantly. "But he's been real grumpy since you guys got back from the Bahamas."

"Any idea what's wrong?"

"Well, I do know two things that are bothering him."

"Talk."

"Your trip was a disaster. I learned that from the newspaper. All Danny told me was that there were two terrible accidents."

"Accidents my foot, two people were murdered."

"Really," Greg said. "The newspaper said one."

"Yes, well, the cops don't want the public to know everything. What's the second thing that's bothering Danny?"

"Several people have seen you cruising around town with Cliffview's richest, most eligible bachelor. Of course, they ran right in here to tell Danny. He tried not to show it, but he was very upset."

"Cliffview's most eligible bachelor?" I was mystified. "Who's that?"

"Tony d'Argent."

"You know I work part-time for the Cliffview PD. Since the chief's on vacation Tony's been supervising me. Besides, while he's most certainly attractive and a bachelor he's a cop so he can't be rich."

Greg raised an eyebrow. "You don't know much about him, do you?

"I know nothing about him. Enlighten me."

"His mother is a descendant of a man who owned a huge rancho in Ojai," Greg said. "She inherited a sizable chunk of the property. She and her husband, Charles, opened a spa and built a hotel. Now there's a golf course, equestrian center and tennis courts."

The light dawned. "Tony's family *owns* the Golden Oak Resort and Spa. No wonder his mother's birthday party will be held there. I've been asked to photograph it."

"Danny's not thrilled about your part-time job, Cinnamon, and you wandering around in the middle of the night with a good looking rich guy isn't helping."

That was irritating. "Tony and I rarely 'wander around in the middle of the night.' Mostly we wander around in broad daylight, which is why so damn many people have seen us.

"Danny has no reason to be jealous." I was warming to my subject. "And actually, I'm the one who should be jealous. All women fall in love with their instructors. Danny's had his share of adoring students, indeed, an affair with one of them broke up his marriage."

"If I were you, I wouldn't mention that," Greg advised, "Danny's more than a little sensitive about it."

"I know, I know. I'm just venting."

I thanked Greg and left Cliffview Divers. I knew what was wrong between Danny and me, now I had to figure out what to do about it.

Danny was teaching a scuba class at the pool that evening. I knew he'd have to drop equipment off at his shop afterward. I parked behind Cliffview Divers just after 10:00 and waited. He drove into the lot a short time later. I got out of my car and walked over to where he was unloading gear.

"We need to talk, Danny."

"Not tonight, Cinnamon," he said, not looking at me. "It's late and I'm tired."

His back was toward me. I went over and put my arms around his waist. "I miss you Danny."

He stood very still and stiff, then snorted. "Ha. From what I hear you haven't been lonesome." He didn't turn around.

"If you're talking about Lt. d'Argent you're way off base, Danny. That's work."

"Everybody in town seems to have seen you together. Each and every one of them has dropped by to tell me about it. And I, of course, have no idea what's going on."

"You would if you'd returned my calls." I lifted his arm up and moved under it so I was standing in front of him. I put my arms around his neck and pulled his head down, kissing him on his lips.

He resisted for at least 30 seconds. "I'm telling you, that job is trouble," Danny said. I kissed him again. "Let me finish up here. Then, if you don't have any more dead bodies to photograph, we can go to my place."

I ignored his sarcasm and bit back a tart-tongued reply. Instead, I helped him lug scuba gear from his truck to the back of his shop. Later, at his house, we showered together and made love. It was one of the wildest, most passionate sessions we'd ever had. When we finished, Danny rolled over and went to sleep. I couldn't. Things still weren't right between us. There was a sadness about Danny I'd never felt before and our lovemaking had had an edge of desperation.

Chapter 24

On Friday, Sam flew off to spend the weekend with his mother and stepfather in San Francisco; Danny and I spent that night and Saturday night together. He skillfully evaded my attempts at serious talk. I was glad to be spending time with him and afraid to force the issue, telling myself it could wait till our relationship was on more solid footing.

Danny was already gone when I awoke on Sunday, he'd left early to board a dive boat bound for Anacapa Island with his current scuba class. He'd have dinner with his students afterward, picking up Sam at the airport before heading home.

I'd told Danny about my job at the Golden Oak; if it bothered him, he hid it well.

Only 20 miles from Cliffview, Ojai is reached via a curving two-lane mountain road. It's a pretty drive. The road meanders past giant oaks, raspberry fields, citrus and avocado orchards, ranches and farms. The farther east you go, the more rugged the terrain becomes. The road snakes down to Lake Casitas then starts a gentle climb up to Meiners Oak and finally, the Ojai Valley.

A charming artists' haven known for its fabulous spas, Ojai is only a few blocks long. There are about 10,000 residents, though the population swells with tourists in the summer.

The Golden Oak is the valley's most luxurious resort. The rich and famous come here to relax and pamper themselves with mud baths, horseback riding, tennis and golf as well as the world famous cuisine prepared in the resort's two restaurants.

I gave my name at the gated entrance and was told to park in a specific lot and go to the Ojai Room in the main building.

Tony hurried over as soon as I appeared in the doorway. He must have been watching for me. I thought it would be a small family party, but this was a big room. Tony said more than 200 people were expected.

"Let me introduce you to my family." All of them were busy supervising something but immediately took a few seconds off to greet me. I met Tony's mother, Victoria, first. It was hard to believe she was 50, she didn't look that much older than her son. Petite, with long, straight black hair, she had large brown eyes and flawless olive skin. Tony looked a lot like her. She wore a simple silk caftan that was bright green. Diamonds and emeralds sparkled in her ears, around her neck and wrists and on her fingers. She looked fantastic and I told her so.

"Why thank you," she said. "I'm so glad to meet you, Cinnamon. I met your dad when he was mayor of Cliffview. When Tony suggested you photograph my party we all agreed it was a wonderful idea. I don't know why we didn't think of it sooner." She smiled, showing me where Tony had gotten those even white teeth.

Next, Tony introduced his dad, Charles. A tall, slender man with thinning blond hair and impeccable manners, he was immaculate in navy blue slacks and a silk shirt the exact color of his pale blue eyes.

"Happy to meet you, Cinnamon," he said with a slight French accent. He brought my hand to his lips, his eyes scanning my face intently. "I know you are here to work but I hope you will have some fun as well."

Tony's two sisters were last. Both eyed me curiously when we were introduced. Dressed in jeans and T-shirts, they were just leaving to change for the party. Both looked like their dad.

"Don't let Tony work you too hard," one advised me.

"Be sure to sample the buffet," the other said. "We've spent hours on it."

Guests began to arrive and Tony introduced me to a number of those as well. That was a new experience. I don't usually mingle when I'm working; I'm not there to socialize. I was glad I'd worn my best black pantsuit.

Family members accounted for about half of those present. After I'd met a confusing assortment of grandparents, uncles, aunts and cousins, I started taking pictures. I have to say, I worked my butt off. While most of the photos were routine, the kind I've taken hundreds of times, several included Hollywood A-listers posing with the d'Argents. Now that was fun. While Ted and I had met a lot of celebrities in our LA years, none of them had been super stars.

Victoria d'Argent was the queen of the gathering, a role to which she was obviously accustomed. Although her husband remained in the background, he never took his eyes off her.

The champagne flowed and there was a wonderful buffet, followed by a skit depicting the fascinating history of the rancho on which the Golden Oak had been built. The "actors" were family members who, I learned, performed the skit every year on Mrs. d'Argent's birthday. Afterward, there was dancing, with music supplied by a small band.

The traditional cake was brought in and "Happy Birthday," was sung. Soon after, the guests began to drift off. Many, Tony had told me, were staying on the property. The band played on, though the dance floor was nearly empty. I packed my equipment and was about to leave when Tony approached. I'd noticed that while his sisters had dates, he didn't.

"Have time for a dance before you go?" he asked. He looked gorgeous in a white, Spanish style shirt and black slacks. I couldn't refuse.

It was a slow dance and although we were a bit awkward at first, it wasn't long before he was holding me so close I could hardly catch my breath.

The one dance became two. Being in Tony's arms made me feel all tingly. We were alone on the floor, with the band playing just for us, when an image of Danny popped into my head.

"Oh my, I've got to go." I felt flustered and knew my face was flushed.

"Just one more," Tony said.

"I've got a boyfriend."

"Are you engaged?"

"Well, no."

"There you have it." Tony's arm remained firmly around my waist.

"I really have to go," I said, gently putting space between us.

"Some other time, then," he said lightly. "Can I help you with your equipment?"

As I drove off a few minutes later, I looked in the review mirror. Tony was watching me.

Driving down the winding road, now dark, to Cliffview I alternated between warm, fuzzy feelings for Tony and horrible guilt about Danny. At Greene's, I unloaded the truck. I didn't have to download the photos I'd shot of the birthday party just then, but I did anyway. I needed something else to think about.

When the job was done, I was exhausted. I'd been on my feet for several hours and the euphoria caused by the heady dances with Tony had evaporated, leaving me limp with fatigue.

At home in my very quiet condo, I checked for phone messages. There weren't any. I showered and fell into bed.

Chapter 25

Guilt and damage control propelled me to seek out Danny the next day. I bought a large sub sandwich at the supermarket deli and took it and a quart of Diet Coke to his shop shortly before noon. I also brought Dave Pecot's logbook.

Danny wasn't overjoyed to see me. He seemed tired and said he hadn't slept well. That was unusual, Danny can sleep through almost anything.

"Difficult class yesterday?" I probed.

"No. They were fine. I certified all of them, first time around."

"Sam okay?"

"Yeah, he's fine."

He didn't elaborate, so I told him about my job the day before, mentioning that I'd danced with Tony. I figured I'd better tell him before somebody else did. There was no reaction. Danny was definitely distracted.

Then I said, "I got an e-mail and a package from Mac."

Danny perked up. Not a lot, but a little. "Oh?" he said.

I told him Mac's theory that the dolphins that had brought Tom to us were escapees from the Oceanarium in Freeport, then added, "Mac also sent me Dave's logbook. A diver found it in the sand on the Sugar Wreck. Mac dried it out in the engine room. He thinks I should give it to Dave's widow. If you have her phone number I'll make arrangements to do that."

I took the logbook out of the envelope and set it on the desk in front of Danny.

Danny picked up the logbook gingerly. "Oh shit," he said. "Poor Dave. Shouldn't this go to the police?"

"I thought about that," I said. "After looking through it, I don't think so. It's just a boring recitation of the creatures Dave saw on his dives, including the depth at which they were sighted. I can't imagine that would be much use to the police. Especially since Dave was killed above water."

Danny ran a finger over Dave's name on the cover and said, half to himself, "It would devastate him to see it now. David F. Pecot, rest in peace."

He picked up the log and examined the cover more closely. "That's odd. I'm pretty sure Dave's middle name was Irwin. Someone changed the gold 'I' to an 'F' with a black pen."

"How strange," I said. "Why would anyone do that?"

"I have no idea," Danny said, putting the log down. He stood and went over to a file cabinet, pulling out the top drawer. A minute later, he held a Manila file folder labeled "Bahamas Trip." He flipped through it, retrieving a single sheet of paper, which he handed to me. It was the form Dave had filled out, listing his name, address, phone number, certification card number, passport number and other vital information. Danny handed it to me. I'd completed one just like it before our trip. Under "middle name," Dave had written "Irwin."

"I'll go with you when you give the log to Laura," Danny said. "It's the least I can do. Is tonight okay?"

That was fine with me. Danny called Mrs. Pecot, telling her only that the two of us wanted to give her something of Dave's that had just been found.

A few minutes later, I was on my way back to Greene's, feeling slightly depressed. Danny had been so remote.

We had dinner that night at the Pizza Den, Sam's favorite eatery. Danny remained preoccupied. His participation in the conversation was sporadic. Sam didn't seem to notice. He talked nearly nonstop about what he'd done in school that day, then segued onto the preparations his mother and stepfather were making for the twins. He had brought his mother's latest ultrasound to show me.

Sam and I huddled over the ultrasound, the edges of which were a bit tattered. Sam showed each one he got to everyone he knew. While I'd seen several of Sandy's, I wasn't that good at deciphering them.

"These are the babies," Sam told me. "The girl is Jenna and this is my brother, Adam. You can tell he's a boy by this." He pointed to a tiny object on the ultrasound and giggled.

"Oh my," I said. "That is most definitely a boy. Have you seen this, Danny?"

"Several dozen times," Danny said.

"Dad and Sandy haven't decided what to name my brother yet," I told Sam. "But I kinda like the name Tyler."

"Me too," Sam said. "Hey. You're lots older than your brother." He chuckled. "Old enough to be his mom."

"No way," I said. "I'm way too young to be a mom." I meant it as a joke, one that was lost on the Decker males.

"No you aren't," Sam said.

"He's right," Danny said. "Actually, you're getting kinda old to have babies."

His words had an undertone of bitterness. I looked at him, surprised. "I've got lots of time left."

"The years pass quickly," Danny said.

"They do," Sam agreed. "I'll be nine in a few months."

After dinner, we dropped Sam off at Danny's house and, when the babysitter arrived, headed for the Pecot residence in Ventura. The trip through the cool foggy evening was made in silence. I don't know what occupied Danny's thoughts but I was mulling over the marriage and baby issues.

Several years ago Danny had been left a small inheritance by a distant relative. He used it to fulfill his dream of owning a dive store. That caused a rift between him and his wife; she wanted a house and another child. Danny spent a great deal of time at the shop learning the business and the rift widened. It became impossibly deep when his wife discovered Danny was having an affair with one of his students.

Although the affair was brief, the damage had been done. Danny's wife filed for divorce. Deprived of the family he'd ignored, Danny realized how much they meant to him. He was devastated when the ex-wife quickly remarried and moved to San Francisco, taking Sam with her.

When she got pregnant with twins and was confined to bed, she sent Sam to live with Danny until the babies were born. I wondered if Danny was unhappily anticipating the end of that arrangement.

He'd told me about his affair, claiming he'd learned his lesson. If he ever "tied the knot" again, he said, he'd walk the straight and narrow. He'd also made several references to having more kids. Although he hadn't come right out and said so, I was pretty sure it was me he wanted to have those kids with.

That was a problem. I really loved Danny. I was, however, newly divorced and not ready to contemplate a second marriage. Kids, should I decide to have them, seemed far in the future.

The Pecots lived in the mountains of Ventura near the church where Dave had worked. Temple Crystal was a magnificent white marble edifice illuminated at night by a thousand lights. Seeing it now, all I could think of was how huge the electric bill must be.

The Pecot residence was also impressive; it looked like something from the cover of Architectural Digest. A multi-level structure, it was perched on a mountainside.

Laura Pecot answered the door. She was gorgeous even in jeans and a T-shirt. A profound sadness enveloped her like a cloud.

She invited us in, leading us to the living room where she suggested we have a seat. First, however, Danny and I made a beeline for the floor to ceiling windows. Fog shrouded the hillside below, making it seem as if we were all alone on a pinnacle in the sky.

"Can I offer you something to drink?" Laura asked.

"No thanks," I said, adding, "I am very sorry for your loss. I only knew Dave a few days but I liked him a lot. He was great fun. I can't believe he's gone."

"It's been a horrible shock," Laura said. "I don't know if I'll ever get over it. I've known him since I was three. We were very close."

I removed the logbook from its envelope and held it out to Mrs. Pecot. "We kidded him about all the time he spent writing in this, but we knew he treasured it. It was found on the bottom of the ocean last week. The captain of the boat asked us to give it to you."

Laura took the book from me and glanced at the cover, then took a step backward and dropped it. Clasping her hands firmly together in front of her, she made a visible effort to compose herself before speaking.

"I didn't participate in that part of my husband's life," she said. "The log means nothing to me. Why don't you give it to Mike? He went on those trips with Dave."

She made no move to pick up the logbook, leaving that to me. As I put the book back in the envelope I said, "I'll ask Mike if he wants it."

We stood there awkwardly until Danny said, "We should go.

Sorry about Dave."

"You have our sympathy," I said. "He was a great guy."

We were headed toward the front door when Laura said, "I almost forgot. I found a camera in Dave's luggage that wasn't his. Maybe you can find out who it belongs to."

She went over to a credenza near the door and picked up a small point and shoot camera. I knew whose it was as soon as I laid eyes on it.

"That's mine," I told her. "I've looked all over for it. Thank you so much." Impulsively, I took a couple of steps forward and hugged Laura, who stood as still as a statue.

Danny and I said good-bye and left. Back in his truck, I said, "Was that strange or what?"

"Very strange," Danny confirmed. "I got the impression Laura was jealous of the time Dave spent with Mike."

"That was my take, too," I said.

In the car, I turned on my camera and tried to view the photos that should have been in it. The camera claimed the memory card was empty.

"Someone erased the images."

"You're sure they were erased?"

"Absolutely. They're probably not gone forever, though. I have a software program that should restore them."

We drove in silence for a while then Danny asked, "Would you mind taking the logbook to Mike? I don't want to go."

"Sure," I said.

At his house, we watched the news on TV. Or rather, I did. Danny disappeared and didn't return. When the news ended, I found him in bed, sound asleep. This was most unlike Danny. I was puzzled by his actions and deeply hurt. I showered and lay down beside him, my anger building minute by minute. Finally, I could take it no loner. I sat up and turned on the light.

"Wake up, Danny," I demanded. "We have to talk."

"Not tonight," Danny pulled the covers over his head.

"Yes tonight. Now."

"No."

"If you won't talk to me, I'm leaving."

"Suit yourself."

Madder than the Mad Hatter, I dressed and let myself out. I wanted to slam the door but didn't because it might wake Sam.

It wasn't until I stood alone on the cold dark street that I realized I hadn't driven to Danny's and had no car. No way would I go back inside that house. Beside, my condo was less than two miles away. I headed home at a brisk jog.

I hadn't gone far before tears began spilling down my cheeks. I was on the Highway 101 overpass when a Cliffview PD black and white drew alongside me. I glanced at it and kept going. The officer inside the car lowered the passenger side window.

"You okay Cinnamon?" he yelled.

I was mortified he knew my name and hoped he couldn't see my tear-streaked face. I didn't look at him when I said, "I'm fine."

"I'd be happy to give you a lift."

"Go away," I yelled. But he continued to tag along behind me. I ran as fast as I could. The sooner I got home, the sooner this nightmare would end.

By the time I reached the shopping mall that contained Greene's One Stop Camera and Photo Shop, my hurt at Danny's actions had turned to anger. This was all his fault. If he had just agreed to talk to me I wouldn't be jogging down the street in the dark of night followed by a police car. Who the hell did he think he was, anyway?

A block from my condo, the anger dissipated, replaced by exhaustion. I wasn't used to running so fast, so far.

As I trudged up the stairs, I glanced behind me. The black and white was parked at the curb, engine idling.

Physically and emotionally drained, I dropped, fully clothed, into bed.

The doorbell rang. I dragged myself to the door.

"Who's there?" I demanded. It better not be a cop.

"It's me," Danny said in a low voice. "I'm sorry. I was way out of line. Please let me in."

"No," I said. "Not tonight. Maybe not ever." I didn't really mean that last part, of course, but it gave me great satisfaction to say it. I went back to bed and fell asleep instantly.

Chapter 26

Danny called the next morning. I let voice mail pick it up. When he called me later at Greene's, I refused to talk to him. When he resorted to e-mail, I opened and read his messages but didn't reply. My anger, however, had evaporated. I resisted the impulse to phone him simply because it was too soon to give in.

Instead, I used the software that restored deleted images to memory cards. Whoever erased them probably had no idea they weren't gone forever.

It worked. The software restored all but one of the images. Six were of Tom's body. The close-ups I'd taken of Tom's neck clearly showed the marks made by the ligature.

I found Detective Gray's card and dialed his number. He wasn't there, so I left a message telling him the missing camera had been found and I would be happy to send him the images I had of Tom. I left my cell phone number in case he wanted to call me.

Then I phoned Tony, asking if he'd look at the photos and tell me if my interpretation of them was accurate. He said he'd drop by after his shift ended.

I had a lot to do at work and the hours went fast. Before I knew it, the other employees were gone. I was alone in the store when Tony arrived. He had showered, shaved and dressed in clean jeans and an open necked sport shirt. He looked terrific and seemed happy to see me. I felt rumpled and a bit skuzzy in the clothes I'd worn on a busy day.

We went back to my office. There, he moved a chair next to mine and we sat side by side. I was very much aware how close he was. I brought the photos up on my computer screen.

"You're right on, Cinnamon. Those are definitely ligature marks. Tom was strangled. Want to tell me what happened over a drink?"

I said yes, half hoping someone would see us together and tell Danny about it. Revenge is always good for the soul.

Not long afterward we were parking in the lot of Cliffview's newest restaurant, which also has the darkest, most romantic bar in town. It was crowded with couples. Conversation was next to impossible over the buzz. We had nearly finished one drink when Tony asked, "How about dinner?"

"Fine," I said. "But it's probably too late to get a table here."

"I'll ask anyway," Tony said. He pushed his way through the crowded room and returned with a smiling hostess a few minutes later. To my surprise, she led us to a very private booth in a quiet corner.

"How did you do that? Danny and I tried to get reservations and were told the place was booked two weeks ahead."

"The owner used to work at the Golden Oak."

The table was lit by one small candle. Tony ordered a bottle of wine and I began telling him about our disastrous Bahamas trip. He listened attentively, asking occasional questions. Caught up in my narrative, I ordered a meal and ate it without really tasting anything. Once the waiter had removed my plate, I couldn't remember what I'd had. I'd also consumed more than my usual one or two glasses of wine.

When I finally finished telling my tale, Tony asked, "So, who do you think killed Tom? Someone with both motive and opportunity."

"I don't know. Nobody on the boat liked him. He irritated and annoyed crew and passengers alike. But the trip would have been over in a few days, so why kill him? I have no idea what the motive was. Opportunity is easier but no less problematical. Everybody, including me, had opportunity."

I had talked about a lot of people and Tony was having a trouble keeping track of all of them. On a napkin, I made a list of those on the boat:

"Tom Tiburon: murder victim, fraternity brother of Dave and Mike, former boyfriend of Jessica.

"Kimberly Tiburon: Tom's wife of three years.

"Dave Pecot: possible murder victim. Mike Keating's best friend/dive buddy of many years. Found in the walk-in freezer next to Tom. Fraternity brother of Mike and Tom.

"Mike Keating: Dave Pecot's best friend. Fraternity brother of Dave and Tom.

"Paul Patterson: Cliffview Chronicle publisher, no known ties to Tom.

"Cathy Doherty: Paul's girlfriend, no known ties to Tom.

"Pete Johnson: former marine, retired Cliffview High PE teacher, boyfriend of Jessica, who got dumped by Tom.

"Jessica Wheeler: preschool teacher, Pete's girlfriend, dated Tom in high school.

"Red Greene: no ties to Tom.

"Sandy Greene: no ties to Tom.

"Cinnamon Greene: absolutely no ties to Tom.

"Capt. Mac: knew Tom from past encounters.

"Danny Decker: organizer of Bahamas trip, no ties to Tom.

"DD II crew: second skipper, divemaster and two cooks, no known ties to Tom."

I pointed out that the people who had known Tom before the trip had kept that a secret. And that Dave was probably killed because he knew who had strangled Tom.

We'd finished our meal and were sipping coffee. The restaurant had grown quiet and when I looked around, I noticed only two other tables were occupied.

"Let's approach this from another angle," Tony suggested. "Who would you rule out?"

I took my pen and put an X before the names of the *DD II* crew members, myself, Danny, Dad, Sandy, Paul, Cathy, Jessica and Kimberly.

"Why eliminate the wife?" Tony asked. "I'd consider her the number one suspect."

"I don't think she has the mental or physical strength," I explained. The look on his face prompted me to ask, "Do you know her?"

"Yes," Tony said. "I worked the death of her mother-in-law, Martha Martin."

"So you met both Tom and Kimberly," I said.

Tony nodded.

"Jessica said Martha's death was ruled an accident but some thought she committed suicide," I said. "Is that true?"

"Yes."

"I've heard the blue ringed octopus is toxic," I said.

"Extremely toxic. I consulted a marine biologist at UC Santa Barbara. He told me it only takes one bite. The toxin works fast, causing respiratory distress and cardiac arrest.

"It's not the bite that was the problem, however. It's how she got it. This is an animal the size of a golf ball. It was used to being handfed by Martha. Yet she was found with the octopus in her hand, crushed. No one could believe she would do that."

Tony thought for a moment before continuing. "She was in excellent health and seemed happy. She had plenty of money. If she had any serious problems, she kept them to herself.

"There was no note and no evidence at all to suggest it was suicide."

"You had doubts."

"A lot of them. According to Martha's staff, she rarely stayed late and had no reason to do so that night. She also had no reason to put her hand in the octopus tank. The animal had been fed earlier that day.

"And then there's this: Blue ringed octopus have a lifespan of 18 months. Hers was a bit older than that."

"It was dying and she chose to die with it," I said.

"Possibly," Tony said. "There was no way to prove that, though."

"Were Kimberly and Tom married when Martha died?" I asked.

"They were engaged."

"How did he react?"

"He was devastated. My gut told me his grief was genuine."

"How about Kimberly?"

"She pretended to be upset. I thought it was an act. There was no love lost between her and Martha. Her mother-in-law to be wanted Kimberly to sign a prenup."

"Surely Tom would have insisted on that anyway."

"Not necessarily. This was his first marriage and he thought it would last forever. According to him, he and Kimberly were soul mates."

"And mom was skeptical."

"You bet," Tony said. "Tom's inheritance was substantial. There was a lot of money involved."

"Did you consider murder?"

"Of course," Tony said. "That was even harder to prove than suicide. Tom had no motive. He and his mother seemed to have a very solid relationship. Besides, his dad left him a fortune, he didn't need his mother's much smaller estate.

"Kimberly was the only person who might have benefited from the death. With no Martha there would be no prenup."

I thought back to the urn incident during Tom's memorial service. "I have seen Kimberly really angry," I admitted. "But murder? As I already said, I don't think she has the physical or mental strength."

"I think she's much more complex and capable than she appears. Also, I don't think there's any doubt she married Tom for his money. But you're right, I don't see her as a murderer. And if she did kill her future mother-in-law it was counterproductive. Tom had a prenup drawn up after his mother died simply because she had wanted him to have one."

Cliffview restaurants don't stay open late. The staff of this one was already cleaning part of the room. We were the only customers. Tony glanced around then said, "Why don't we continue this at my place?"

That gave me pause for thought. Although I had avoided talking to Danny, I was planning to forgive him soon. While I hoped he'd find out I'd had dinner with Tony and suffer a little bit (or maybe a lot), I didn't want to irreparably damage our relationship. And I didn't want to be tempted to do so.

"I can't stay long, I've got an early morning appointment," I lied.

Chapter 27

Tony's condo was right on the beach. He drove us there in his shiny new sports car, which he parked in the subterranean garage. We took the elevator to the third floor.

I was expecting a typical bachelor pad; lots of black leather and chrome with a pool table and/or a huge screen TV as the focal point. I was stunned when Tony led me into a spacious living room with a tasteful Southwestern decor. The dominant color was white, with pastel blue and mauve accents. The floors were wood and ceramic tile with area rugs. There were plants everywhere and they were live ones, not maintenance-free faux plants.

"Wow," I said. "This is beautiful."

Tony looked pleased. "One of my sisters is an interior designer and she helped me get the look I wanted."

"Does she take care of the plants?" I asked.

Tony laughed. "Nope. That's my territory. I inherited my mom's green thumb. I've always had lots of plants. I minored in horticulture in college."

He led me out on the balcony that ran the length of his bedroom and living room. It contained even more plants. They hung from the roof in baskets and lined the base of the railing in pots.

The view was gorgeous. The night sky was clear; the offshore oilrigs were all lit up and sparkling like Christmas trees.

A cool breeze blew off the ocean and I shivered.

"Cold?" Tony put an arm around my shoulder.

Warning bells went off in my head. Romantic balconies are dangerous.

"Let's finish our discussion inside," I said.

Seated on the white couch, I took the cocktail napkin list out of my purse. "Where were we?"

"We were talking about suspects," Tony reminded me. "We'd just finished with Kimberly. Tell me about the other people on your trip."

I looked at my list. "Dad and Sandy are definitely not suspects," I said.

"No bias there," Tony commented, grinning. "One's your dad, the other your stepmother. There is such as thing as being too close to an investigation, Cinnamon."

"I know, but neither of them had any real problems with Tom."

"Okay, that's a legitimate reason. Go on."

"Jessica isn't a suspect. Although it hurt when Tom dumped her, it happened a long time ago. She thinks he's a jerk now. Plus, she seems very happy with Pete."

"What do you know about him?" Tony asked.

"He was a Cliffview High PE teacher for 20 years," I said. "And he's a member of the Wednesday Warriors, a group Dad, Sandy, Danny and I dive with once a month. I've known him for years but I don't really know him. He seems to be a straight arrow kind of guy. Since he was in the military, however, he'd probably be familiar with a garrote."

"Good point. Now, why eliminate the boat crew?"

"Because dead divers are bad for business. Capt. Mac would never jeopardize future charters by killing someone during a trip. Plus, his big bad captain act is just that, an act.

"Besides, the crew didn't seem all that bothered by Tom," I continued. "I'm sure they've dealt with obnoxious passengers before and they'd know it was only a matter of days before he'd be gone. They'd have no reason to murder him."

Tony consulted my list. "How about Cathy, Paul and Danny?" he asked.

"You know Paul and Cathy," I said. "Can you imagine either of them murdering anyone?"

Tony laughed. "Not in a million years. Let's talk about Danny."

"Danny wouldn't harm a flea," I said, suddenly defensive.

"According to what you've told me, Danny was upset with Tom for several reasons." Tony said, ticking them off on the fingers of one hand. "Number one: Tom was ruining your trip by being nasty to guests and crew and not following the rules. Number two: Tom scared away the dolphins you'd come to see. Number three: Tom threatened you after you dived with Kimberly. You indicated that

Danny would have gone after Tom at that point if you hadn't stopped him."

"Yeah, but...." I began.

Tony interrupted me. "Number four, you and Danny haven't been getting along since you returned from the Bahamas. So something is bothering him. Maybe that something is murder."

"How do you know we're not getting along?"

"It's true isn't it?"

"Well yes. But how did you know? I don't appreciate people prying into my personal life." I stood up, ready to stalk out.

"I haven't been prying. The officer who followed you home last night told me about it."

"Oh." The anger evaporated and I sat down. Tears stung my eyes.

"Can I get you something to drink?" Tony asked gently. "Wine, beer, water, Diet Coke or juice?"

"Diet Coke," I said. "A Diet Coke would be good."

Tony busied himself in the kitchen while I composed myself. When he returned, he carried two glasses and handed one to me.

"That's enough serious stuff for one night. Let's do something fun. Do you play cards?"

So, for the next 45 minutes, we sat at his kitchen table and played double solitaire. Tony is competitive, aggressive and has incredible reflexes. He easily won the first three fast-paced games. I won a couple of the games that followed, enjoying them immensely. Concentrating on the cards, I forgot about Danny and the murders. I laughed a lot and relaxed.

Around midnight, fatigue hit. I looked at my watch. "I've got to go. My carriage will be turning into a pumpkin any minute now."

"Okay. I'll take you home."

As we stepped on the elevator, he draped an arm around my shoulder. This time I left it there.

Tony drove the few blocks to my house and walked me to my door. I thought he'd try to kiss me and wasn't sure what I'd do if he did. All I got, however, was a brotherly peck on the cheek. He wished me "Good night" as he went down the stairs and didn't look back.

I have to admit, I was disappointed.

Chapter 28

The phone rang too early the next morning. "This better be important," I grumped.

"Breakfast at The Bakery?" Danny asked.

Since I hadn't decided when to end his punishment, I didn't answer right away.

"Cinnamon? Are you there?"

"Give me 20?" I said, making a decision and finding my voice.

"See you soon."

He showed up earlier than I expected. When I opened the door he looked so unsure of his reception that I couldn't help myself. I pulled him inside and stepped into his arms before he had time to utter a word. Not long afterward we were literally rolling around in the throes of passion. I abandoned myself to it and was breathless when we finished.

"That's another apology," Danny said. "Sorry. I've got a lot of stuff on my mind these days."

"Exactly what is all that 'stuff?'"

"I'll tell you at breakfast."

Holding hands, we walked the four blocks to The Bakery, which is in the same small mall as Greene's One Stop Camera Shop.

It was a beautiful day, with a bright, fiery sun in a clear blue sky. A light breeze blew off the ocean.

"Where's Sam?" I asked.

"Friend's house for a sleepover," Danny said. "Where were you last night? I called and left you a voice mail."

"I was out," I said, stalling for time. I had gone out with Tony to punish Danny. Now that we'd made up, it seemed childish.

"I know. I came by to see if you were there and just not answering the phone," Danny said. "Your condo was dark. Red didn't know where you were either."

"Dad's not my social secretary," I said, bristling. "I don't check with him before I go places." What was I going to tell him?

"So where were you?"

"Out."

"Where?" Danny persisted.

I sighed. He'd hear about it soon enough as it was. Somebody was bound to have seen Tony and me last night.

"The camera Laura Pecot found in Dave's luggage was the one that contained the photos of Tom's body. I wanted Tony to see them. We were only going to have a drink afterward but ended up having dinner."

"Oh. What did Tony think of the pictures?"

I didn't like the emphasis he put on "Tony."

"He agrees with me that there are ligature marks on Tom's neck. We discussed who might have killed him."

"Sounds like loads of fun," Danny said sarcastically.

"It was thought-provoking. Afterward, we played double solitaire."

"What an exciting evening." It was said in jealousy and I wasn't going to let him get away with it.

"Tony is excellent company," I shot back. "And I didn't have to run home in the dark at the end of the evening, he drove me to my apartment in his car."

"Ouch" Danny grimaced. He paused a moment, then continued. "Let's start over. What are you going to have for breakfast?"

We talked about safe subjects till we got to The Bakery. The wonderful aromas emanating from the kitchen had my mouth watering long before I ordered a large vanilla nut coffee and a chocolate muffin filled with cream cheese. Danny had a cinnamon roll and a latte.

We carried our food and drinks to the patio. I love having breakfast there. The flowering vines on the latticework had just been misted and were still damp; the enclosure exuded peace and quiet.

When we got to the patio, however, we found Dad, Sandy, Paul and Cathy seated at a large table.

"Come join us," came a nearly simultaneous chorus. So much for an intimate conversation with Danny. The six of us spent the next 45 minutes talking about nearly everything except what I had hoped to discuss.

The patio filled up as we lingered over a second cup of coffee. At one point, someone touched my shoulder lightly. I looked up to see Tony, apparently on his way out. I hadn't noticed him come in. Standing next to him was an attractive dark haired woman I'd never seen before.

"Hi Tony," I said brightly, nearly knocking over my coffee cup. Then I asked, "Does everyone know Tony d'Argent?"

Everyone said "yes" but Danny. He stood, introduced himself to Tony and the two men shook hands. It was anything but friendly, they appeared to be sizing each other up. Tony introduced the woman with him as his cousin Luisa. Then he said, "Nice to see you," winked at me and left.

"How do you like working with Tony?" Cathy asked, proving once again that the Cliffview Chronicle's society columnist knew everything that was happening in our town, no matter how minor.

"He's very helpful and informative so I'm finally learning how to do the job," I said. "The chief gives orders and never explains anything."

"Lucky girl," Cathy said, "Tony's a hunk." When I frowned, her face turned pink and she turned to Danny, adding, "Not that Cinnamon could possibly be interested in Tony when she has you."

The group broke up shortly after that. Sandy said she had to show a house; Paul and Cathy said they were expecting company; Danny said he needed to pick up Sam and Dad reminded me we were due at Greene's.

Danny kissed me before heading off. "I'll call you later," he said.

Dad and I walked the few doors to Greene's together.

"So, everything's okay between you and Danny?" he asked.

"No," I said. "We were supposed to have a serious talk over breakfast. As you can probably guess, that didn't happen."

I told him about my dinner with Tony. "He's helping me figure out who murdered Tom, and possibly Dave. But I don't agree with everything he says. He considers Danny a suspect."

"Well that's ridiculous," Dad said. Then he chuckled. "But that explains the tension between them. Well, Danny could use a little competition. Make him treat my little girl right." He kissed the top of my head.

"Oh Dad," I said, rolling my eyes.

"Oh Cinnamon," he said, mocking me.

The day was very busy. I had an octogenarian birthday luncheon to video at noon and a kid's birthday party to video after that. I didn't get back to Greene's until closing time. Among my telephone messages were a couple from Danny and one from Tony. I called Danny first.

"Cinnamon, at last."

I explained what I'd been doing all day.

"You've earned a reward," Danny said. "How about dinner and a movie in Santa Barbara? I've got a sitter lined up for Sam."

He said he'd pick me up at 7:00 and hung up. Next I called Tony. He answered on the first ring.

We chatted a bit then he said, "I found your cocktail napkin suspect list this morning and realized we never got around to discussing two of the people on it. And I'd like to know more about Dave Pecot's death. Do you have time for dinner or lunch in the next couple of days?"

"Lunch would be good." I didn't say dinner might be dangerous.

"Day after tomorrow?" Tony asked. "Eleven-thirty?"

"Day after tomorrow it is."

I took special care getting ready for dinner with Danny that night. After showering, I selected my best pair of jeans and a new, dark purple cotton sweater. I slid the golden dolphin earrings Danny had given me into my ears.

The jeans had been washed but not worn since the Bahamas trip. I felt a lump in one of the pockets that turned out to be a ball of crumpled paper. I unfolded it. The paper was torn in such a way that the two lines of small printing on it were illegible with the exception of two words: "blame me." This was the scrap Danny and I had found as we were leaving the *DD II* in Miami.

The doorbell rang and I stuffed the paper back into my pocket. When I opened the door, Danny stood there, wearing that evil grin I like so much. It was one I hadn't seen for awhile.

Danny's short brown curly hair was still a little damp and he smelled of coconut shampoo. He wore an open necked shirt the same dark blue as his eyes.

He grabbed me and long, passionate kiss followed. I'd missed those. If we hadn't had dinner reservations, a lot more would have transpired.

As we drove the 10 minutes north to Santa Barbara, we talked about the day and what we'd done. Danny got off the 101 at Cabrillo and followed it past Stearns Wharf to the harbor parking lot. Our destination was a rectangular two story building on the waterfront. White, with a red tile roof, it houses two restaurants and a maritime museum.

We parked in the lot and walked through the night to the restaurant. Evenings warm enough to go without a jacket are infrequent here and this was one of them. The sky was clear, the wind barely a whisper.

The waterfront leading to our destination was labeled Fish Walk and contained several plaques describing the history of Santa Barbara's fishing industry.

Danny and I come here several times a year. The grill on the top floor is casual, with excellent, not-too-expensive fare. The restaurant on the first floor draws a somewhat better dressed crowd with deeper pockets. The view from both is outstanding.

Small fishing boats dock just below Fish Walk; dive boats are found at the easternmost section of the marina at Sea Landing. That's the home of the *California Diver*, host of our Wednesday Warrior trips.

Serving as a backdrop, the lights from incredibly expensive houses twinkle on the mountainsides surrounding the harbor.

In the second floor restaurant we were seated at a table overlooking the water.

We ordered a bottle of inexpensive white wine. As we were sipping our first glass, I said, "Did I tell you the police escorted me home the other night?"

Danny colored. "I realized you didn't have your car shortly after you left. I jumped in my truck and went after you. So yes, I saw the cop.

"Yesterday, several people asked me why you were running down the street in the middle of the night with the police following you."

"What did you tell them?"

"Nothing. I acted surprised."

"I'm jogging home from your place late at night and you claim not to know anything about it?" I asked. "Fat chance."

"That's my story and I'm sticking to it. Can we move on here?"

"Oh," I said. "Remember that piece of paper with 'blame me' written on it? I found it my pocket tonight. It went through the washer and dryer in my jeans."

My jeans are a tight fit and I had to stand up to retrieve the paper, which I placed on the table. Danny smoothed it out with his fingers.

"It feels like waterproof paper," he said. "Probably from somebody's dive logbook."

The same idea hit us both.

"Dave Pecot's logbook," I said. "I haven't had a chance to take it to Mike, I still have it at home. That minuscule printing looks like Dave's. I wonder what it means?"

Neither of us had a clue.

Several times during our meal I thought of reminding Danny we were supposed to have a talk at breakfast that morning. The time never seemed right, though.

Afterward, we went to a movie in downtown Santa Barbara. It was a romantic comedy, which I love and Danny usually avoids. That he suggested and suffered through it, gritting his teeth only occasionally, showed me how hard he was trying to make things right between us. At his place afterward, our lovemaking was intense. But once again, I felt an edge of desperation and a sadness I didn't understand at all.

Chapter 29

I called Mike Keating at his law office the next morning. I said I needed to talk to him and, although he pressed me for details, I was evasive. I hadn't intended to be that way, it just happened. Mike gave me his home address and said I could stop by after 8:00 pm.

I also called Mrs. d'Argent. The proofs from her birthday party had been ready for days. I'd had prints made of her with all of the celebrities and shown them to the staff members at Greene's, who were suitably impressed.

"I'd give an arm and a leg to work with you on one of these parties," Dad said, "How about suggesting they hire me to do a video next time? I'd love meeting some of those people."

Mrs. d'Argent must have been really busy because it took her awhile to settle on a time and date to view the photos. She put me on hold twice before she finally said, "I'm afraid all I've got open is Friday at 4:30. How does that sound?"

I checked my calendar. "That would be fine."

"Since the appointment is so late, why don't you have dinner with Charles and me afterward?"

Of course I agreed.

"Excellent," she said, sounding very pleased. "Have you seen the resort grounds?"

When I answered in the negative, she said, "I'll arrange a tour of the Golden Oak for you as well."

That appointment made Friday night something to look forward to. The Golden Oak's restaurants are world-renowned and the resort would be gorgeous at night.

I was so excited I actually skipped down the hall to Dad's office to tell him about it. A little smirk danced at the corners of his mouth. "So mom has been recruited," he said, partly to himself.

"What does that mean?"

"Never mind, honey. Did I tell you the two of us are shooting a photo of the new Chamber of Commerce officers tomorrow?"

Danny dropped by in the middle of the afternoon, bringing two lattes from The Bakery. He said he had a new scuba certification class starting that night. Then he asked, "Are you going on the Wednesday Warriors dive?"

The Warriors is a loosely organized group of about 30 people who go out on the *California Diver* one Wednesday a month. Dad and Sandy are regulars, as are Paul and Pete. Several people had skipped recent trips: Sandy wouldn't be diving until after the baby was born and Dad and I had been too busy.

"I'd love to go."

"I'll call you after my class," Danny said, "and you can tell me about your visit with Mike."

Mike had said, "anytime after 8:00." I got there a few minutes early. He lived in the nicest section of Camarillo, just a few miles east of Oxnard and about 30 minutes from Cliffview.

GPS flawlessly directed me to the Keatings' large, two story house, which looked well maintained in the streetlight. A dark blue SUV and a silver sports car were parked in the driveway.

I rang the doorbell. A slender, dark haired woman answered the door.

"I'm Cinnamon Greene. I'm here to see Mike."

"Come on in. He's on the phone. I'm Barbara."

Neat as a pin in a pair of jeans and a red turtleneck sweater, she led me to the living room.

"Have a seat," Barbara said, indicating a craftsmen style sofa. "He shouldn't be too long."

I settled onto the sofa. Barbara started to leave, then changed her mind and perched on the arm at one end. She seemed uncomfortable.

"Mike told us so much about you that I feel I already know you, Burgie," I said.

The woman frowned. "I much prefer my given name."

"Sorry, Barbara." I was surprised by her tone. Both Mike and Dave had referred to her as "Burgie." I'd assumed it was an oft-used nickname.

The voices of two boys drifted down from upstairs.

I made another attempt at conversation. "Mike showed us photos of your boys, they're very handsome. How old are they?"

She smiled briefly. "Thirteen and nine."

"Do you work outside the home?" I asked.

"I guess you don't know as much about me as you think," Barbara said. "I'm a lawyer, like my husband."

Wow. She was downright snippy. I was mystified by her attitude. "Do you and Mike work for the same company?" I asked.

"Heavens no. Mike specializes in family law, mainly divorces, I'm in medical malpractice," she said.

To my relief, Mike arrived just then. I couldn't have put up with Barbara's hostility much longer without exhibiting a little of my own.

Mike flopped down in a chair opposite us. He looked tired and grouchy. He wore a faded pair of navy blue sweatpants, a gray sweatshirt and no shoes. One of his socks had a hole in the toe. He wasted no time on pleasantries.

"What did you want to see me about?"

I had been planning to lead up to the logbook by explaining how and when it was found but the Keatings were so rude I cut right to the chase. I pulled the logbook from the envelope and offered it to Mike.

"Mac sent this to me," I said. "He asked me to give it to Laura Pecot. She thought you'd appreciate it more."

Mike started to reach for the book, then hesitated, the color draining from his face. He looked as if he'd seen a ghost. He sucked in a breath and said, "I don't want the damn thing. Throw it back in the ocean." He pushed himself out of the chair and strode from the room.

I sat in stunned silence for a few seconds. When I regained my composure, I asked, "What just happened?"

Barbara had been staring at the doorway her husband had just gone through. She looked at me as if I were an alien. "Go home."

I opened my mouth to protest, then closed it. I slipped the logbook back in the envelope and made my way out. I heard Barbara lock the door behind me.

I paused on the doorstep, wondering what the hell was going on. The Mike I'd known on the trip and the one I'd just seen were two different people. I liked the first one a whole lot better.

As I drove home, I thought about Mike's parting comment. "Throw it back in the ocean," he'd said. Since I hadn't mentioned where the logbook was found, how did he know?

Chapter 30

I was in bed, reading Tony Hillerman's memoir, *Seldom Disappointed*, when Danny called. I told him what had happened at Mike's house.

"This just gets stranger and stranger. I don't know what to make of it."

"That makes two of us."

"Did you compare the 'blame me' scrap to pages in Dave's logbook?" Danny asked.

"Yes. The paper, handwriting and ink look identical."

"Any idea what it means?"

"None whatsoever."

Tuesday morning passed in a blur of activity. I was editing the videos taken on Sunday when Miguel Takamura stuck his head in the door.

"You've got a visitor."

Puzzled, I followed him to the showroom where I found Tony chatting with Dad. When he saw me he smiled and tapped his watch, "You forgot, didn't you?"

"Forgot what?"

"Lunch?"

"Oh," I said. "Sorry. Give me a couple of minutes."

"We can do it another day."

"No, no. Today is fine."

Tony suggested the small French restaurant Paris, which was near his condo. It's in the same strip mall as the Pizza Den, where Danny, Sam and I have spent many an evening.

We walked the four blocks west from small mall to smaller mall along the town's main street, Cliffview Avenue. The morning fog had yet to dissipate; the air was cool and damp. My sinuses loved it.

I, however, didn't love the attention that Tony, wearing his CPD uniform, attracted. All who passed eyed us curiously. Many greeted him by name. A few even said "hello" to me.

Danny probably knew all about our walk long before we got to the restaurant.

The staff of Paris was delighted to see Tony. He was, it seems, a frequent customer.

"My dad is French, as I'm sure you realize," explained, "and he thinks this is the best French restaurant in the area. The prices are reasonable, too."

Well, maybe they were reasonable to Tony. They seemed a trifle high to someone who exists, for the most part, on fast food.

Our waitress was super nice to my companion. She ignored me.

Tony was right about the cuisine. Over an excellent spinach/mushroom/cheese quiche and brewed, not instant, iced tea, I told Tony what I knew about Dave and Mike, along with the finding of Dave's logbook and the scrap of "blame me" paper.

"You're sure it's from Dave's log?" Tony's face wore an expression I hadn't seen before.

"Positive," I said, then had an idea. "Do you think you could have it and the log fingerprinted?"

Tony hesitated then said, "If I had elimination prints, sure, I probably could. I'm amazed you would ask me, though. Those two items are evidence in a murder investigation. You need to send them to the Miami cops, along with a note telling them what you just told me."

I flushed and dropped my eyes. Although I knew Tony was right, I didn't like the tone of his voice.

"The log is as boring as hell," I said, more than a little defensive. "It's just a list of creatures Dave saw underwater and exactly where he saw them."

"But the note was probably torn out of it. That makes it something the police need to investigate, not you. FedEx those things to Miami. The sooner the better."

By the time he finished, my ears were burning. Later, walking back to Greene's, we had little to say to each other and completed the trip in silence.

"Thanks for lunch," I said, unenthusiastically.

"You're welcome. Don't forget what I told you."

Yeah, well, that would have to wait. The two items in question were at my condo. By the time I got home, it was be too late to ship them anywhere and I had a Wednesday Warriors trip the next day. Since I couldn't send the items to Miami until after the trip, I decided to take them with me. Three people hadn't been pleased to see the log. Paul and Pete would probably be on the Warriors trip, what would be the harm in seeing their reactions?

I packed swimsuit, towel, sweatshirt, toiletries and topside camera equipment. If the weather permitted we'd be going to Santa Barbara Island, home of friendly sea lions, so I decided to take my underwater camera system. Then I went to bed. My dive gear was stored at Danny's shop and he'd bring it with him in the morning.

The alarm went off at 5:30 am; Danny arrived at 6:00. It was a chilly morning. We drove to the boat without speaking, breakfasting on the French roast coffee and fresh cinnamon rolls Danny had gotten at The Bakery before he picked me up.

When all our gear had been stowed aboard the *California Diver*, we retired to the bunkroom. I was soon asleep, snuggled up next to Danny, feeling warm and comfortable.

I awoke several hours later to find Danny gone. The engines were off and the boat rocked on choppy seas. I could hear the steady drone of the generator. I sat up slowly, then rolled out of the bunk. The other bunks were already empty.

Up on deck, people were returning from the first dive. There would be at least three more dives, so I had plenty of time to get ready. Since neither Danny nor Dad was on the deck, I figured they must be in the water.

The boat was anchored off Santa Barbara, one of California's eight Channel Islands. Five of them, including Santa Barbara, form the Channel Islands National Park and Marine Sanctuary.

The sky was heavily overcast and a light, cold wind blew across the stern. In the distance, white caps topped the waves. I shivered and zipped up my hooded sweatshirt as I went into the galley to get a cup of coffee.

Dad and Danny came in about 15 minutes later. They both wore knee length windbreakers over their wetsuits and their faces were red. Stirring his cup of hot chocolate, Danny said, "I won't lie to you, it's nasty down there."

"The water temperature is in the low 50s, the visibility is about 15 feet and there's surge down to 60 feet," Dad added.

Paul Patterson joined us. "Not a day for a delicate damsel,

Cinnamon," he informed me. "Curl up in a warm bunk and forget about diving today."

The "delicate damsel" appellation was intended to goad me into proving I wasn't one. As usual, I rose to the challenge. We were moving to a new site where the conditions might be better. There was a good chance of seeing one or more playful sea lions. I might even get a lobster or two. I decided to make one dive. If I didn't like it, I didn't have to make another. I did, however, leave my underwater camera system packed in its case. I didn't think the visibility would improve enough to use it.

I assembled my equipment and pulled on my wetsuit as the boat weighed anchor and moved to a second spot. Danny and I made the next dive together.

After a tropical vacation, the first California dive is always a little difficult. I'd gotten used to warm water, a thinner, more flexible wetsuit, not wearing a hood and carrying less weight. In my coldwater gear, I felt heavy and awkward.

The dive wasn't a whole lot of fun. We didn't see anything noteworthy. When we got above 60 feet the surge tossed us about and we got separated a couple of times in the ten-foot visibility. About 15 minutes into the dive, after Danny disappeared in yet another sandstorm, I'd had it. When we finally found each other, I indicated "up" and Danny led the way back to the boat. We surfaced to find the wind had picked up.

"That's it for me," I told Danny. On the deck, I stripped off my wetsuit, stowed my gear and made my shivery way below decks. The rocking of the boat made showering and getting dressed difficult. Back in the galley, I learned that 20 of the 25 divers aboard had voted to end the diving day early. We were headed home.

The size of the seas was not conducive to socializing in the galley. Almost everyone retired to his or her bunk. My plan to show the logbook to Pete and Paul was forgotten.

We returned to Cliffview earlier than usual. In the back room of Danny's dive shop, we rinsed our gear and hung it up to dry. One of the perks of dating Danny is that my bathtub and balcony don't have to be used for this task. And, when everything is dry, Danny stores it in one of his lockers.

When we finished taking care of our gear, we talked to Greg for a while before closing time. "Sam and I are going to McDonald's tonight," Danny told me, "want to come?"

"Sure." The cupboards were pretty bare at home.

Since I didn't want to leave my cameras in the car while we were in the restaurant, we locked them in Danny's back room. His shop has an alarm system.

McDonald's was full of parents and kids. We shared a table with two other couples Danny knew. Once they had their food, the kids roamed around, never spending as long as a minute in one place. The din was horrible. Conversation was possible only if you shouted. Sam and his friends bounced off the walls while Danny and the couples at our table discussed soccer teams and the PTA.

Afterward, as Danny drove me home, an over-stimulated Sam excitedly related every single thing he'd done that day. I developed a splitting headache.

Danny parked in front of my building, then he and Sam walked me upstairs. I was surprised to find the door to my place slightly ajar. When I pushed it open I discovered my condo had been trashed.

Chapter 31

"Oh shit," I said. The condo looked as if it had been hit by a tornado. Danny, Sam and I walked through the three rooms, noting the devastation. Drawers had been pulled out and their contents dumped on the floor. The sheets and blankets had been ripped from the bed; the mattress and box spring overturned. Clothes from the closet were tossed haphazardly about.

Even the refrigerator had been vandalized. Luckily, there hadn't been much in it. The orange juice carton was empty, its contents poured into the sink, and the former occupants of the freezer, a large but nearly empty container of chocolate chunk ice cream and two ice cube trays, had been dumped on the floor, where they'd melted into small and, in the case of the ice cream, sticky, puddles.

"What a mess," Sam said.

"Why would anyone do this?" I asked Danny. There was a knot in my stomach and I was close to tears.

"I don't know, Sunshine," Danny said. He put an arm around me, then pulled out his cell phone. "I'm calling the cops."

My condo is less than a mile from the station. Two officers I knew by sight but not by name arrived a few minutes later and introduced themselves. When I started to tell them my name one of them said, "You and I met a couple of nights ago, Cinnamon."

"We did?" I stared at him uncomprehendingly.

"You were jogging along Cliffview Boulevard," he reminded me, a broad grin spreading across his face.

"Oh," I said, flushing. I glanced at Danny, who also turned red.

While Danny, Sam and I waited, the two officers went through the rooms. When they finished, they asked me what was missing. I don't own much of value other than camera and dive equipment and most of that was at Danny's store. The small point and shoot camera

I keep in my condo had been liberated from its case but not stolen.

"I don't think anything is missing," I said.

"Are you sure?" asked the cop who had followed me home.

"I can't be positive," I said. "Things aren't in their normal places. But they didn't take my camera or jewelry." The box I kept the latter in had been emptied onto the dresser top but everything seemed to be there, albeit in a tangled mess. I picked out my most treasured pieces: the emerald pendant from Dad and Sandy and two pairs of earrings from Danny.

"What about drugs?" one cop asked. "Any prescription bottles missing?"

"I don't take any," I said.

Now I felt insulted. Didn't I have anything worth stealing?

"Nothing's missing," I said. "Nothing at all."

"Maybe it's just a case of malicious mischief then," one of the officers commented. "You been having trouble with anyone?"

"No," I said.

"No disputes with anybody about anything? No personnel problems at work?"

"Absolutely none," I said, adding, "How did they get in? I locked the door when I left and all of the windows are still closed and locked."

"Anybody have a key besides you?" one of the cops asked.

"The condo manager and Danny," I said.

"I have mine," Danny said, holding up his key ring.

"Where were you...." one of the cops started to ask Danny.

"He picked me up at 6:00 this morning. We've been together all day," I said.

"Just checking," the cop said. "We'll talk to the manager, see if someone borrowed his key, but most probably the lock was picked."

"I've got a deadbolt," I pointed out.

"Thieves can open almost anything given enough time," the officer said.

Tony arrived just then. He's one of two Cliffview cops who also function as criminalists. This was the first time I'd seen him since our lunch and he was once again the consummate professional. You'd never guess we'd ever met. He set about dusting for and collecting fingerprints while the first two officers began interviewing my neighbors, who were milling around in the hall outside my door.

Later I'd learn the only unusual thing anyone had seen were two men wearing blue jumpsuits with the logo of an air conditioning company on them. That was odd because there are no air conditioning units in my building — it rarely gets hot enough to use them in Cliffview.

After the cops left, I called Dad to tell him what had happened. He was properly horrified.

"I'll come get you," he said.

"No, no," I told him. "There isn't anything you can do and besides, Danny and Sam are here. I'm going home with them. I will need tomorrow off so I can clean up this mess."

Dad agreed and we disconnected.

I selected a change of clothes from the garments strewn on the floor and left with Danny and Sam.

Chapter 32

On the way to Danny's I said, "The cops asked if I was having trouble with anyone, I told them 'no.' Am I missing something?"

"If you are, I'm missing it, too," Danny admitted. "You don't have any enemies I know of."

"Me either," Sam said. His big eyes and ears had been taking in everything. "Everybody I know likes you."

"Thanks," I said. He can be a pretty cool little guy.

It had been a very long day and I was dead tired, but once in bed, I couldn't sleep. Every time I closed my eyes, I saw the chaos in my condo. I wracked my brain trying to think of a reason someone would trash my home.

I didn't want to wake Danny with my tossing and turning so I went into the living room, where, huddled under a blanket, I watched TV with the sound muted till the sky began to lighten.

Danny dropped me at my condo on his way to work. I told him he didn't need to see me to the door but I guess I protested too much and he thought I wanted him to. He walked through the place, making sure no criminals were lurking in the closets, before heading off to Cliffview Divers.

My first priority was to restore order and scrub away all evidence that someone had invaded my space. I had only been home a few minutes when the doorbell rang.

"Who's there?" I asked, with trepidation, though I know thieves don't ring doorbells.

"It's the clean-up crew," two female voices chorused. Sandy and Cathy Doherty had come to help. They wore huge smiles and work clothes consisting of sweatpants and oversized T-shirts. I invited them in and gave both a hug.

The three of us divided up the chores. My first job was to wash my clothes and bedding. I piled everything in a laundry basket and rode the elevator down to the laundry room in the subterranean garage.

I loaded two washing machines, added liquid soap and fed them quarters. As I walked back to the elevator, which was right next to my parking space, I glanced at my truck.

"Shit," I said out loud. The driver side door was slightly open.

I don't keep much personal stuff in the truck but it does contain Cliffview PD's cameras, strobes and lenses. The latter are in an insulated heavy-duty steel case bolted to the car's frame and secured with special locks. The case showed signs of tampering but its security hadn't been breached. When I opened it, everything was untouched. My CDs, however, littered the floor of the cab.

Back in my condo, I told Sandy and Cathy about the truck and then called Cliffview PD, asking for Tony. He met me in the garage about ten minutes later.

"It doesn't make any sense," I told him. "Nothing was taken from my truck or condo."

"Whoever did this was looking for something," Tony commented. "I don't think they found it."

"Maybe it's a case of mistaken identity," I said, warming to the idea.

"If it was the condo or the truck alone, maybe," Tony said. "But both were searched. That tells me there was a specific target."

"This is really unnerving," I said. "I feel very insecure."

"It might take you a while to get over it," Tony agreed. "Cliffview PD will help by keeping an eye on your place. Someone will drive by on a regular basis, day and night. If you want us to check on you personally, we can do that, too."

"Thanks," I said.

Tony made a little bow. "Cliffview's finest at your service, ma'am. By the way, can I offer you a ride tomorrow afternoon? I've been appointed your Golden Oak tour guide."

I had to think a minute. A lot had happened since I made the appointment to show Mrs. d'Argent her birthday party photos.

"Sure," I said.

"Pick you up at 3:30. Don't forget, you're having dinner with us."

He got ready to do some fingerprinting as I took the elevator up to my condo.

Sandy and Cathy had accomplished quite a lot while I was gone, now they cleaned while I straightened and put things away. Soon the condo was neat as a pin, a most unusual state of affairs.

Sandy had claimed the kitchen as her territory. At one point, she opened my refrigerator. "Aha," she announced. "I know what they stole." Cathy and I crowded around her.

"What?" I asked.

"Your food," Sandy said, "they cleaned out your refrigerator."

"Not true," I said. "The essentials are still here: margarine, mustard, mayonnaise, cheese, peanut butter and two sesame seed bagels."

"Doesn't look like my fridge," Cathy observed. "But then you don't look like me, either." She patted her ample hips. "Maybe I should try the empty fridge diet." She picked up the chunk of cheese and examined it. "You need to throw this away. There's something growing on it."

"There goes lunch," Sandy said.

"We still have bagels," I pointed out.

"Let's order Chinese take-out," Sandy suggested.

I called our order in, then went down to the laundry room and put my stuff in the dryers. Tony was getting ready to leave.

"Find anything?"

"Lots of prints. But they're probably all yours. Anybody other than you and Red use the truck?"

"No," I said. "Danny and Sam have ridden in it, though. And sometimes people help me load or unload equipment when I'm shooting an event."

"We'll need exemplars of everyone you can think of who's been in it, so we can eliminate their prints." He wrote down the names I gave him and left.

Later, over fried rice, orange chicken and broccoli beef. Sandy, Cathy and I discussed the Wednesday Warriors' trip I had made the previous day.

"Paul told me how rough it was," Cathy said, using chopsticks to plop a chunk of chicken in her mouth. "Sounded like the hurricane in the Bahamas all over again."

"Not even close to that," I said, "but it wasn't as good as it could have been."

Talking about the trip reminded me of something. I turned to Cathy. "How well do you know Pete?"

"Not very," Cathy said. "He and Paul have been friends for decades but Pete isn't one to share confidences, as I'm sure you've noticed."

"I seem to remember he was a widower when I was in high school and that he had a son and a daughter, both older than me," I said.

"That's true," Cathy said. "The wife died when the kids were teenagers and Pete never remarried. His daughter is in her late thirties, married and has a son. I've seen pictures of her and her family. They live on the East Coast. Pete's son would be about Jessica's age. Pete never mentions him and I think they're estranged."

"I would never have put Pete and Jessica together," I said. "But they seem to get along very well."

"Yes, they do," Cathy said. "They're talking about moving in together, which is a huge step for them."

"You don't think Pete was involved in Tom's or Dave's death, do you?" Sandy asked, scooping up some fried rice with her chopsticks. "I'd bet all that toughness covers a soft center."

"Pete was a marine," I pointed out. "He survived at least one tour of duty during a war. And he can't have liked the way Tom treated Jessica on our trip."

"If Pete got mad enough he might fight with someone," Cathy said. "But murder? I don't think so." She cracked open her fortune cookie and pulled out the little strip of paper inside. "Let's see what old proverb Cliffview's fortune cookie factory has mangled this time," she said. She read her fortune to herself, laughed, then read it out loud: 'The early worm gets the bird.'"

Sandy opened her cookie. "'Every silver lining has a cloud.'"

I opened my cookie. "'He who burns with fire gets played,'" I read. "Now what the heck does that mean?"

Chapter 33

That night was a big test of my courage. I knew whoever had broken into my condo was long gone and wouldn't be back but I still felt very uneasy. Danny thought I should stay with him for a couple of days and Dad and Sandy repeated their offer to put me up. But I knew I had to overcome my fear sooner or later. I chose sooner.

At bedtime, I checked the locks on all the doors three times. When I turned out the lights, however, every sound made the hairs on my arms stand on end and raised utter fear in my heart.

I got up and pushed the sofa in front of the door and turned on a light in the living room. Just before I got back in bed I looked out my bedroom window and saw a Cliffview PD cruiser drive slowly by. That helped a great deal. I fell asleep, awakening to an unusual noise with a rapidly beating heart only a couple of times.

No evil had befallen me when morning came. I took that as a good sign. After the girls left, I had gone to the store to restock my fridge and cupboard. Danny called as I was breakfasting on a chocolate chip bagel, orange juice and coffee.

"Morning, Sunshine. Sleep okay?"

"It wasn't too bad and it should get easier."

"You put the couch in front of the door, didn't you?"

"Yes," I admitted, "How did you know?"

"That's what I would have done. Sam is off to San Francisco this afternoon and tomorrow I'm teaching a refresher course on the *California Diver*. There are spots open if you want to go."

"I believe I'll pass," I said. "Wednesday is still fresh in my mind."

"How about dinner tonight then?" Danny asked.

"I can't. I have an appointment with Mrs. d'Argent this afternoon. She invited me to have dinner with her and her husband afterward."

"Great. I bet Tony will just happen to show up."

"Actually, his mother asked him to give me a ride up there and a tour of the resort. Is that a problem?" I asked.

There was silence for a moment.

"No," Danny sighed. "Forget I said anything. You're a big girl and I have to trust you to do the right thing." He changed the subject. "Did you know your cameras are still in my back room?"

"Yes. Do you need me to pick them up?"

"Any plans for Saturday night?"

"No."

"How about Flanagan's? It's country music night. I can bring your cameras to you when I pick you up."

We set a time and disconnected. Although I kept reminding myself that I was going to the Golden Oak on business, not a date, I dressed with care, choosing my second best black outfit (I'd worn the best one to the birthday party) and slipping the golden seahorses Danny had given me into my ears.

I hadn't been into work for two days. Before I could start on the backlog, however, I had to suffer through the comments made on my attire. Those used to seeing me in slacks and a Greene's polo shirt noticed the wardrobe upgrade immediately.

"Wow. Look at you. Where is Danny taking you tonight?" Miguel Takamura asked.

"Danny is on his own. I'm showing Mrs. d'Argent her photos this afternoon and I've been invited to dinner afterward at The Acorn."

"Will Tony be there?" That came from Julie, our bookkeeper.

"Yes," I said. "His mother asked him to give me a tour of the resort."

"Cinnamon's got a hot date, Cinnamon's got a hot date," Miguel chanted.

"It's not a date, it's business." I was blushing.

"Sure it is," Miguel said.

I fled to my office and spent the rest of the day there and in the video editing room. Before I knew it, Tony was in the showroom, talking to Dad. The rest of the staff concocted excuses to show up there, too, glancing surreptitiously at Tony, who was immaculate in camel colored wool slacks and a black, open necked shirt.

Tony did a double take when I walked into the room. "You look great."

"She does clean up nicely," Dad said, grinning.

"Thanks," I mumbled. Face red, I led the way out of Greene's.

"Everything okay last night?" Tony asked as I climbed into his car.

"It was fine," I said. "Seeing a patrol car go by just before I went to bed helped. Thanks, I owe you."

Tony smiled. "I'll think about the payment."

On the drive to Ojai he asked, "Did you send the logbook to Miami?"

"Shit," I said. "I forgot all about that. I'll do it first thing tomorrow."

At the Golden Oak, Tony parked behind a two-story building, then took me through a back door and down a long corridor to his mother's office. He kissed his mother on the cheek.

"I'll let the two of you get to work," he said. "Call me when you're finished, Mom, and I'll come get her. See you later, Cinnamon."

Mrs. d'Argent's large office was tastefully decorated. The furniture was dark wood, walnut, I think. The walls and carpeting were off-white, the chairs and sofa were upholstered in gold brocade. It was the perfect setting for her. She was stunning in a gold silk pantsuit, her hair pulled back in a bun.

We sat side-by-side at a table in one corner of the room as I showed her the birthday album.

Mrs. d'Argent was very enthusiastic.

"These are amazing," she said. "We've never had a professional photograph any of our family events, we thought it would be too intrusive. We were wrong. I wish we'd done this years ago. The only problem is that there are so many good pictures. It's hard to choose just a few."

As it turned out, she couldn't. I ended up with the largest print order I'd ever written. When we were finished, Mrs. d'Argent called Tony. He showed up a few minutes later.

The tour was conducted via golf cart, the principal means of transportation at the Golden Oak. We started, appropriately enough, on the golf course, which wound up, down and around gentle hills.

As the sun dropped from view, little lights blinked on along the path and the air got chilly. Tony retrieved two jackets with Golden Oak logos from the back of the cart and helped me into one before putting on the other.

As he drove, Tony provided a colorful account of his boyhood on the property.

"Did you go to school in Ojai?" I asked.

"We had private classes here, all the way through high school," Tony said. "My parents were worried we'd be kidnapped like Patty Hearst."

The tour took us past two very large freeform swimming pools, each set amid lush landscaping. We also saw the stables and six lighted tennis courts, all of which were busy.

We finally returned to the main building, which housed the resort offices, the reception area and the two restaurants, the Acorn and the Oak Leaf. Tony parked opposite the hotel in a lot designed for golf carts. We walked across the street and wandered through the beautiful, fragrant gardens surrounding the hotel.

"Why did you become a cop?" I asked. "Surely your parents would like to have you involved here."

"My sisters and I will inherit the Golden Oak. We've been preparing for that all of our lives. Growing up my parents made sure we had a variety of jobs. Mucking out the stables, life guarding at the pool, waiting tables, we did a little of everything. Along the way, my sisters found things they really enjoyed doing. The youngest is the Acorn's sous chef; my other sister is the resort's interior designer.

"Unfortunately, I haven't been able to find a niche. Maybe it's because as long as I can remember, I've wanted to be a cop. Not a big city cop, a small city cop. I love my job in Cliffview. I hope to be chief there someday."

"I could hardly wait to leave Cliffview," I said. "Then I spent eight years in Hollywood. The first few were exciting. Ted and I went to dozens of parties and met a lot of celebrities. We never made any real friends, though.

"When my marriage ended I really didn't want to move back to Cliffview, there just didn't seem to be any other choice at the time. Now, I have to admit I like living there. The air is clean, it's much less crowded and I have friends and family I can count on.

"If I didn't appreciate that before the break-in, I sure do now. I also appreciate a police force that keeps an eye on my condo at night. Can't see LAPD having the manpower, the time or the desire to do that," I said, winding down at last.

We had stopped walking and stood in front of the Spanish style fountain in the courtyard of the hotel. Tony draped an arm over my shoulder and reached into his pocket with his other hand to pull out two pennies. "Make a wish, Cinnamon," he said, handing me one and tossing the other into the fountain.

I had to think before throwing mine. Several things in my life needed fixing, it was hard to pick just one. I settled on wishing Danny and I could be happy again, like we were before the Bahamas trip. Maybe that wish was meant to make me feel less guilty about spending time with somebody else.

After I flipped my penny into the fountain. Tony said, "Let's go eat."

Inside the restaurant, we were shown to a table for four next to a window overlooking the courtyard we'd just left. It was an extraordinarily romantic setting. Water from the fountain tinkled soothingly. The atmosphere was hushed and serene.

Mr. and Mrs. d'Argent joined us a few minutes later. She was vivacious in a red silk dress. He was dapper in navy blue slacks and a blue silk shirt.

"Do you prefer red or white wine, Cinnamon?" Mr. d'Argent asked.

"White," I said.

A waiter materialized and d'Argent ordered two bottles of wine, one red and one white, as well as an appetizer. He didn't consult the menu.

In fact, I noticed, I was the only one given a menu.

"What do you recommend?" I asked.

The d'Argents looked pleased and Tony winked at me. I gathered I'd asked the right question.

"I recommend letting Charles order, the restaurant is his domain," Mrs. d'Argent said, "and I'm sure he's got something special planned for us."

"Great," I said.

When the waiter returned, Mr. d'Argent ordered for all of us.

We made short work of the appetizer, which was vegetables tempura. They were hot and crisp, cooked tableside as we watched.

We were sipping wine and enjoying a salad of walnuts, radicchio and various other exotic lettuces, orange sections and Gorgonzola cheese, when Tony frowned and pulled a cell phone from a pouch on his belt. He opened it, spoke his name, listened and said "Okay. I'm leaving now."

He stood up. "Sorry everybody. I've got to go back to Cliffview."

"I'll go with you," I said.

"No," he said and was gone. I was more than a little put out by his abrupt departure.

"Don't mind Tony, he's always doing that," Mrs. d'Argent said. "Be glad you aren't going with him. He drives like a mad man on those narrow, twisty roads. I'm always afraid he's going to crash."

"I have no way to get home."

"We'll take care of that," Mrs. d'Argent told me. "Maybe you'd like to spend the night here. You could have a soothing soak in our spa, relax and pamper yourself a bit. I'm sure Tony will be here to drive you home after breakfast."

It was a very tempting offer but it didn't feel right.

"I'd better go home. I have things to do early tomorrow."

"Are you sure?"

"Yes."

The rest of the meal was delightful. The food was excellent and the d'Argents, very charming. I heard several anecdotes about Tony and his sisters and we gossiped about current events in Cliffview.

As we were leaving the Acorn, Mrs. d'Argent again suggested I spend the night at the Golden Oak. Again, I demurred. In the lobby of the hotel, Charles d'Argent bid me good-bye, kissing me on both cheeks and telling me how much he enjoyed meeting me.

"We must do this again soon, Cinnamon."

Mrs. d'Argent had gone off to speak to the concierge.

"Your driver will be here momentarily," she said when she returned. She and I chatted for about five minutes, then a man in a well-pressed black suit, crisp white shirt, black tie and highly polished black shoes walked up.

"Cinnamon, this is Arturo," Mrs. d'Argent said. "Arturo, Please take Ms Greene anywhere she wants to go."

To me she said, "Have fun and do come visit us again soon."

Arturo led the way to a white stretch limousine parked in the driveway outside the lobby. He opened one of the back doors, motioned me inside, then closed the door and walked around to the driver's side. From behind the steering wheel he asked, "Where to, Miss?"

I gave him my address and sat back, feeling the way Cinderella must have felt the first night she danced with the prince.

"Holy shit," I said, half to myself, looking around and marveling.

I saw the driver smile in the rearview mirror. "There's a mini-bar and snacks if you're interested," he said.

I'd just had a wonderful meal and wasn't hungry or thirsty. An opportunity like this, however, might never come again. The mini-bar was well stocked. I found a small bottle of champagne with a twist off lid and poured it into a glass. As the limousine wound down the hills to Cliffview I sipped the bubbly and nibbled on salted cashews. I could get used to this.

I had hoped at least one person would see me alight from the limousine and be escorted to my condo door by its driver, but alas, as near as I could tell, there were no witnesses. The ride-induced euphoria (or perhaps it was the champagne) left a smile on my lips as I fell asleep.

Chapter 34

The front door was locked and the showroom was empty when I got to Greene's a few minutes late the next day. I was surprised and disoriented. Was it a holiday?

The store wasn't deserted, though, the entire staff was gathered around the TV in the break room.

"Cinnamon," Dad said. He was very excited. "Were you there?"

"Where?"

"At the motel with Tony," he said. "You know, the guy holding his family hostage. The one Lawson and Tony talked into surrendering right here in front of us."

"What are you talking about?"

Dad and Miguel filled me in. It seems a man with a gun had holed up in a Cliffview motel with his wife and two young children, threatening to kill them and himself. The standoff had lasted all through the night and was just ending. Chief Lawson and Tony had managed to talk the man into letting his family leave and Tony eventually persuaded him to give up his gun and come outside. As I watched, the man, who was lying face down on the sidewalk, was handcuffed and put into a police car.

The on-camera reporter made a big deal out of the fact that not a shot had been fired. She advised us that even though the station was going back to its regular programming, periodic updates would be posted on their website.

"Whew. That was really something." Dad turned off the TV. "The chief and Tony are heroes. Too bad you didn't get to see them in action."

"So, how did your date go?" Miguel asked as we walked down the hall toward the showroom.

"It wasn't a date," I said, annoyed. "I got a huge print order from Mrs. d'Argent, then had dinner with her and her husband. Tony got a phone call and left while we were eating our salads. He didn't say why. Mrs. d'Argent sent me home in a stretch limo."

"A stretch limo?" Dad said from behind us.

"I drank champagne in it," I said.

"That's nice," Miguel said. "But you weren't at the motel?"

"No," I said.

My second in the spotlight was over. I went into my office. The first of three portrait sittings was scheduled to begin in ten minutes.

That afternoon, Dad and I worked a small wedding. He dropped me at my condo afterward. My cell phone rang as I unlocked the door.

"My house was tossed while I was out on the boat today," Danny told me. "Nothing was taken. Chief Lawson thinks it was the same people who did yours, two men wearing blue jumpsuits with the name of an air conditioning company on them. Sam's babysitter, Sara, saw them crossing the street. She didn't see where they came from or where they went."

"That's bizarre," I said. "What do we have that anyone wants?"

"Don't know. Sara, her mom and Sam are helping me clean up the mess. We're almost finished. I'll pick you up in about an hour, okay?"

I had just finished blow-drying my hair when the doorbell rang. Expecting Danny I opened it. Instead, Tony stood there. He wore his uniform and was probably headed for the station. He appeared exceptionally cheerful.

"You got home okay?"

"Yes," I said. "In a luxurious stretch limo."

"I'm sorry I had to leave."

"It's okay. I heard what happened."

Danny showed up just then. His face wore a scowl, something I've seen on it only rarely.

"Ready to go, Cinnamon?" he glared at Tony.

"Just checking to make sure you got home okay," Tony said. "See you Cinnamon. Hello to you, too, Danny." He turned and walked down the stairs.

"Thanks for the evening," I yelled after him, mostly for Danny's benefit.

As promised, Danny had brought the camera equipment I'd left in his office after our boat trip. As he set them down in my living room, I remembered the log and the scrap of paper were in one of them. Oh shit. Well, I'd send them to Miami tomorrow. Meanwhile, there were people I wanted to show those items to and some might be at Flanagan's. I took the manila envelope out of the camera bag.

"Let's just see what sort of reaction this causes in the rest of the group," I told Danny, tucking it under my arm.

While Danny hadn't asked me what had happened at the Golden Oak I knew he was dying to know. On the way to Flanagan's I told him. He tried to suppress a grin when he heard Tony had left early and I'd come home alone.

Flanagan's is the local watering hole. In the summer it's full of tourists and the townspeople avoid it. In the fall, however, the locals reclaim it. On Saturdays there's a music theme and a buffet. Tonight there'd be a DJ playing country music, along with barbecued tri-tip, beans and salad.

The place was noisy and crowded. Danny and I joined Dad, Sandy, Pete, Jessica, Cathy and Paul at a table in one corner of the room.

After Danny poured us beer from a pitcher on the table, we got in line for the buffet. After eating, we line danced and Texas two stepped until the DJ took a break. Lots of people went outside to cool off or smoke and the room finally got quiet enough for conversation.

I took the log and the scrap of paper out of the manila envelope and put them on the table. "Anybody recognize these?" I asked. Nobody gasped or turned white, there was only puzzlement and curiosity on the faces around me.

Paul Patterson spoke first. "That's Dave Pecot's log. How did you get it?"

I told him, adding, "What's strange is that the 'I' on the cover had been changed to an 'F.'"

"What a mean thing to do," Cathy said. "That was Dave's pride and joy."

"'F' stands for fagot," Pete said.

All eyes turned to him.

"Mike and Dave were fairies. I knew it the minute I laid eyes on them. Tom knew it, too."

"I don't believe it," Cathy said. "They're both married."

"That's just for show," Pete said. "Chances are their wives have no idea."

"You have to forgive him someday," Jessica said, so softly only Pete and I heard her.

Pete didn't answer. Instead he said, "I'm getting another pitcher." He grabbed an empty beer pitcher and stood up so quickly he almost knocked his chair over. He stalked over to the bar.

"I still don't believe it," Cathy said.

"Even if it's true, who cares? It's none of our business," Sandy said. "And I would appreciate it if you didn't use those words around me, Pete. I find them offensive."

Heads nodded agreement.

I pointed to the scrap of "blame me" paper and asked if anyone had seen it before. Nobody seemed at all interested in it. I put the log and the paper back in the manila envelope and borrowed Danny's keys so I could lock the envelope in his truck.

The rest of the evening passed without incident. We had a great time. Since Danny had to be up early the next day, he and I were the first to leave. We went to his place, where we showered together, then enjoyed a leisurely love making session that was almost like old times. When I fell asleep, it was definitely Danny who danced through my dreams.

Chapter 35

Danny was gone when I opened my eyes and I hadn't heard a thing. He left me a pot of coffee and a bagel. I ate breakfast while perusing the Sunday paper and enjoying the solitude. Since I didn't have my truck, I walked to work, a distance of just less than two miles. The day was on the brisk side. The ocean breeze ruffled my hair and blew clouds around in the sky. The leaves of eucalyptus trees rustled, giving off a scent reminiscent of bay leaves.

Business was nearly nonexistent. I don't know where the good citizens of Cliffview were but they weren't at Greene's that day. I found a FedEx box and put the log and the scrap of paper in it. On my computer, I composed a long note to Detective Gray telling him everything I knew about both items. I apologized for not sending them to him earlier.

I had just finished the note when Tony called and said he'd be by to pick me up, there was a crime scene to photograph. I was outside waiting when he parked in front of the store. I got into his car.

"We have to go to my condo first," I said. "The cameras are in my truck. What's up?"

"A body on the beach," Tony said. "A couple walking their dog found it about an hour ago."

Cliffview is famous for its broad, sandy shoreline. The aptly named Beach Street runs the length of it, feeding a series of blacktopped parking lots.

The body had washed up just beyond the northernmost lot. A couple of black and whites were already parked at the far end of the lot and yellow tape had been used to cordon off the crime scene. A small crowd had gathered.

Tony parked his car next to the other two and we walked the

several hundred yards to the body. The ocean was all churned up; even in this shallow bay there were white caps. The body was partially covered by damp sand a few feet above the surfline. I figured it had been deposited there during high tide.

When we got close, I saw that the long hair I initially thought was blond was gray. The victim was a tiny old woman, perhaps in her 70s or 80s. She was on her side, facing the ocean, and tangled hair covered her face. She wore jeans and a pale blue sweatshirt. One of her white tennis shoes was missing.

I waited a few feet away while Tony examined the scene. He explained what he wanted and I went to work, photographing the body from several angles, then the face, neck and hands.

Afterward, Tony used oversized tweezers to pick up several items, putting them in paper bags.

The coroner arrived a few minutes later. Tony and the officers conferred with him in voices so low I couldn't hear what they said.

We waited while the coroner examined the body. He secured plastic bags around the woman's hands and her feet, then turned the body over. Tony asked me to take some more photos, which I did.

Afterward, we walked back to Tony's car in silence. As we dumped sand from our shoes and brushed it off our socks, we watched the coroner and another man wrap the body in translucent plastic, then put it on a gurney and carry it back to their vehicle.

"You recognized her, didn't you?" I asked.

"It's Ginnie Martin, Tom Tiburon's grandmother," Tony said. "I think I told you I interviewed her three years ago, when her daughter Martha died."

That news was stunning; I was speechless for several minutes. When I found my voice I asked, "How did she die?"

"She probably drowned," Tony said. "But she didn't go into the water willingly. There were scratches on her arms. She put up a fight. With luck they'll find somebody's DNA under her fingernails."

"People all around Kimberly Tiburon are dying," I said. "Tom, his mother and now his grandmother. Not to mention one of Tom's fraternity brothers. Can all these deaths be coincidental?"

"I'd bet against it," Tony said.

Chapter 36

Back at Greene's, I told Dad about Ginnie Martin. He thought he might have met her at a Cliffview social event but couldn't be sure.

Business did not pick up. I spent some time in my office, puzzling over the deaths of Tom and his grandmother. Maybe her autopsy would provide some clues that would tie all the deaths together.

Danny called late in the afternoon, inviting me to dinner with him and Sam. We arranged to meet at the Pizza Den.

Danny had been pretty much his old self in the past week so I was shocked at his appearance when he and Sam walked into the restaurant. He'd just picked his son up at the airport and should have been happy to have him back. If he was, he sure didn't look it.

Sam pounced upon me, brandishing his mother's latest ultrasound. "Cinnamon, look!" Sometimes the kid talks in exclamation points. "The babies are so big! The doctor says they weigh about four pounds each! They might come early! Mom's got the nursery ready! There's two of everything! I can hardly wait till they get here."

He talked nonstop for several minutes while we ordered pizza and drinks and found a table. When he finally wound down a little, Sam asked, "Can I go play video games?"

Danny gave him a handful of coins and he was off. The Pizza Den has a glassed in soundproof game room, allowing parents to keep an eye on their kids without having to hear them.

Without taking his eyes off his son, Danny drained his beer mug. And I voiced what I finally realized had been bothering him for the last couple of months.

"You were hoping Sam would decide to stay down here and live with you permanently, weren't you?" I asked gently.

Danny gave me a look of pure misery. "I knew it was a long shot. But it's not going to happen. Worse, I'm wondering if he'll even want to come see me after the babies are born. I'm losing him, Cinnamon."

"He loves you, Danny. Of course he'll come see you," I said. But I, too, wondered if that was true. Sam had always wanted siblings. It would be hard for him to tear himself away from the twins, even to visit the father he adored.

We sat without speaking for several minutes, shifting our attention to the TV in the corner since we couldn't think of anything to say. The news was just coming on. The first report concerned the finding of Ginnie Martin's body. "Hey, that's me," I told Danny when a video appeared showing Cliffview PD at work on the beach. The newscaster speculated that the woman had drowned, then added something I didn't know:

"Late this afternoon, the couple's dinghy was found drifting several miles offshore. Inside was the body of Ginnie Martin's husband, George, who was 82.

"Autopsies are pending on both bodies. Sources close to the family said the health of both Martins had been deteriorating recently. There is speculation this was a murder-suicide."

"The Martins were Tom Tiburon's grandparents," I told Danny. "There may be a link between Tom's murder and their deaths."

I didn't get to say anything more because the pizza and Sam arrived simultaneously.

After dinner, the guys walked me to my truck, which was parked next to Danny's. Sam hugged me fiercely before they left, Danny gave me a peck on the cheek. I knew he was upset and distracted. Sam waved as they drove off, Danny didn't. I headed home feeling down.

I didn't sleep well, tossing and turning until the wee hours. There would be a big hole in Danny's life when his son moved back to San Francisco to live with his mother and twin siblings. Danny had already hinted that getting married and having another kid would help fill it.

Therein lay my dilemma. I loved Danny and didn't want to lose him. The thought of marriage and babies, however, made my hair stand on end. I wasn't ready. I wasn't ready at all.

Chapter 37

Weeks passed. I often awoke grouchy, the result of a sleepless night and the conflicts in my life. At Greene's, I holed up in my office. After one look at my dour face, the staff and Dad were more than willing to let me be.

The bright point of several days occurred at 10:00 am one morning, when I opened an e-mail from Capt. Mac.

"Just back from the White Sand Banks," it read. "The Oceanarium's head trainer, Dale, went with us. Several months ago a storm destroyed the gate to the dolphin enclosure. Six dolphins got out. Four came back on their own. Two females didn't. They're the animals that brought Tom to us and we named Notchy and Scratches. They were trained to carry a human on their backs.

"The dolphins were ecstatic about seeing Dale. They did tricks at her command and ate the special treats she'd brought. Although they'd been trained to follow the boat back to Freeport, they disappeared halfway there. Guess they don't want to go back to work.

"Check out the *DD II* website, we've posted pix of the reunion.

"H & K, Mac."

There was also an e-mail from a member of the fraternity Dave, Mike and Tom had belonged to in college. I was pleased about that. I had given up hope that any of the people I'd contacted would reply.

The message was from a man named Larry Walker, who said he'd be happy to talk about his college days. He said he was a past president of the fraternity and had many happy memories to share. He left a phone number with a Los Angeles area code. When I finished answering e-mails, I called him.

Walker explained he was a salesman and spent a lot of time

traveling. He'd just returned from a month long trip and was leaving again soon. We agreed to meet in Santa Monica later that week.

I knew I'd lucked out. Walker loved to talk. It had taken 15 minutes to set up our meeting because he was already reminiscing about what he called "the golden days of my youth." I'd have no trouble getting information out of him, though it might not be exactly what I wanted.

After Walker and I disconnected, I called Tony, hoping for the latest news on the Martin deaths. He was polite but remote, saying he couldn't comment on "an ongoing investigation." That put my nose seriously out of joint.

It was then I remembered I'd never sent Mike's logbook and the scrap of paper to Florida. I couldn't believe I'd forgotten to do that. I'd get another lecture from Tony if he found out and this one would be well deserved. I prepared an air bill and slipped it into the plastic sleeve on the FedEx box I'd left sitting in plain view on a shelf in my office. I was about to seal it when I realized the police would need comparison prints, i.e., exemplars, of the people who had touched the log and possibly the paper. None of us had been fingerprinted in Miami. I was wondering where I might get exemplars when I thought of the forms everyone had completed for Danny before the Bahamas trip. Each of them should have the prints of the person who completed it, along with Danny's.

I wasn't sure Danny would give the forms to me, though. Our relationship had deteriorated. He no longer phoned every day and his call Tuesday afternoon had been short and to the point: "Are you going on the Wednesday Warriors trip?"

The wind had been blowing all week and the water temperature was in the middle 50s.

"No," I said.

"See you."

I knew where the forms were kept and it occurred to me that with Danny out on a boat, I'd have a chance to get them from his office. I agonized over that idea for a while. It would be a serious breach of Danny's trust. Yet the forms contained the only comparison prints I could think of and might be vital to solving Tom's murder.

Besides "borrowing" the forms from Danny's office, I wanted to visit Kimberly Tiburon. I was curious to see her reaction to the death of her husband's grandparents.

Getting the forms proved simple. I dropped by Cliffview Divers just before noon, shot the breeze with Greg Tauchen for a few minutes, then told him I needed to get something from Danny's office. "Have at it," he said. While it wasn't the first time I had done this, Danny had known about the other occasions.

Wearing white cotton gloves I'd brought, I found and copied the forms quickly. I put the copies in the file; the originals went into an envelope I'd brought with me. After saying good-bye to Greg, I added a P.S. to my note to Detective Gray, enclosed the forms and sealed the package. I drove directly to the FedEx office and handed over the package.

Before I left the FedEx lot, I tried to call Kimberly, hoping to set up a visit. However, her landline had been disconnected and there was no referral number. I didn't have her cell phone number and belatedly realized it was probably on the forms I'd just sent to Miami. It was my lunch hour. On the spur of the moment, I decided to pay a visit to the Tiburon mansion.

The security gate was open, so I drove in and parked in the circular driveway. The grounds looked neglected. The grass hadn't been cut recently and was turning brown from lack of water. The bushes needed trimming. There were no lights on in the villa and no one answered repeated ringing of the doorbell and knocking on the front and back doors. The place looked deserted. I wondered where Kimberly was and why no one was taking care of the villa.

Back at Greene's I phoned Cliffview PD, hoping Tony could supply Kimberly's maiden name so I could try and find her family in Santa Monica. He was unavailable.

Okay, I'd have to dig up the information myself. I'd never looked at Tom's website, though I was sure he must have had one. I lucked out. It was still up and the bio page mentioned that he had been married to Kimberly Jensen for three years.

Unfortunately for me, the Jensens are prolific. I found a lot of listings for a lot people with that surname in Santa Monica during an internet search.

I printed out those pages and, even though it was my day off, went into my office at Greene's. There, I started at the top of the list and worked my way to the bottom. If a real person answered, I asked for Kimberly. If a machine answered, I left the following message:

"Hi, Kimberly, this is Cinnamon. Please call me, I need to talk to you." I left both my cell and work numbers.

I went home, did a load of laundry and reconciled my checkbook with several bank statements, keeping an eye on the clock. When I don't go on the Wednesday trips, Danny and I usually have dinner when he gets home. He calls when the boat heads for the mainland after the last dive, somewhere around 3:00. Yet afternoon became early evening and I still hadn't heard from him. My mood changed from one of optimism to one of profound gloom. Perhaps I had better think about Danny and me splitting up.

When the phone rang at 6:30, my heart skipped a beat.

"I've got some good news and some bad news, Cinnamon," Danny said. "The good news is that your dad is going to be okay. The bad news is he got bent rescuing Paul."

Chapter 38

"Dad got bent? How bad is it? Can I see him?"

"He's undergoing treatment in the hyperbaric chamber at Valley View Hospital," Danny said.

"Does Sandy know?"

"No. Can you tell to her? I've got to call Cathy. Can you drive both of them to the hospital?" Danny asked.

He hadn't answered a crucial question. "Is Dad okay?"

"He should be fine. He has a shoulder bends. It's a long story. I'll tell you everything when you get here."

I called Sandy right away. She's a calm, levelheaded person and I thought she took the news well. That was good, because I was falling apart.

By the time I got to her house, however, Sandy had had ten minutes to think about what I'd told her. She was standing in the middle of the street waiting for me and on the verge of hysteria. Must be all those pregnancy hormones.

As soon as I came to a complete stop, Sandy rushed the truck.

"Oh Cinnamon," she wailed. "I'm so scared." I was, too, but I couldn't tell her that. Oddly, the more upset she became, the calmer I got.

"Danny says Dad's going to be okay," I said, trying to sound as if I was sure, which I wasn't.

It took a few minutes to calm Sandy down and get her settled so I could pick up Cathy.

Cathy is also a sensible, levelheaded woman. She was standing on the curb when Sandy and I arrived. While she wasn't hysterical, she was visibly upset. Her "Hi" was tremulous. She dabbed at watery eyes and blew her nose with a seemingly endless supply of tissues pulled from her purse. Somehow I got her into the truck and drove off with the two women huddled together next to me, holding hands and sniffling.

Valley View isn't that far from Cliffview but there was a lot of traffic and it took us twice as long as it should have to get there. No one talked and everyone's anxiety intensified in that time, you could feel it in the air. We all wanted to see for ourselves how the guys were doing.

When we finally arrived at the hospital, I dropped the women off in front and parked the truck in the lot. A few minutes later, I joined Sandy in the hyperbaric unit.

Danny and I had been here before, when one of his student divers was stricken with the bends. We knew that hyperbaric chambers aren't just for scuba diving injuries, they also treat patients with burns, infections, chronic wounds and carbon monoxide poisoning. Most of the latter, however, are treated in much smaller chambers than the nine-foot diameter steel cylinder Dad was in. His injury required longer treatments.

Sandy and the hyperbaric doctor were standing in front of a small port on the side of the chamber and he was explaining what had happened to Dad.

"In the simplest terms," he was saying, "Red was down too deep too long. When he ascended without making a decompression stop, nitrogen dissolved in his tissues at depth came out of solution too fast, forming bubbles that lodged in his shoulder. That caused decompression illness, which you know as the bends.

"To shrink the bubbles so they passed through his system, we put him in the chamber and pressurized him to depth. Now we're slowly bringing him to surface pressure. He's also breathing oxygen most of the time. He's got an break coming up, you can talk to him then."

"Is he going to be okay?" I asked.

"He's doing really, really well," the doctor replied. "His shoulder is greatly improved. He should recover fully though he might need a couple more treatments."

Sandy and I crowded around the port and waved at Dad. He was lying on a gurney with an IV in one arm and an odd-looking mask on his face called a BIBS (Built In Breathing System), through which he was receiving oxygen. He pointed to his shoulder then moved his arm around. The movements looked normal.

While we waited for Dad's air break, the doctor showed us the console that controlled the chamber's various functions. One of the people at the console wore a headset, as did an attendant inside the chamber. The two shared a running commentary.

At the break, the attendant removed Dad's mask and handed him the headset. Sandy used the headset the outside attendant had been wearing. While she and Dad were talking, he slipped off the gurney and walked around.

When the break was over and Dad was once again lying on the gurney wearing the mask, Sandy and I had another chat with the doctor.

"Why does he have an IV?" she asked.

"It's a saline solution for fluid replacement," the doctor said. "He needs to be well hydrated."

"Will there be any lasting effects?" Sandy asked.

"It's too soon to know," the doctor said. "What I can tell you is that we're very happy with his progress."

"What happens when he gets out of the chamber?" Sandy asked.

"You get to take him home. If he needs a follow-up treatment we'll schedule it then."

"Anything special he should do?" Sandy asked.

The doctor shook his head. "Other than take it easy for awhile? No. However, there are things he shouldn't do. No diving, flying or driving to altitudes greater than 3,000 feet until cleared by a doctor."

"How about a cup of coffee? My treat. There's a cafeteria on the third floor."

We'd been so engrossed in what the doctor was saying we hadn't noticed Danny had joined us. He put an arm around my shoulders and kissed me on the cheek. He looked tired and his curly brown hair was stiff with salt.

I put my arms around his waist and hugged him. "How's Paul?"

"Good. Cathy's with him now. She's going to meet us in the cafeteria."

We thanked the doctor before following Danny down the hall to the elevators, which we took to the third floor. The cafeteria was bright and cheerful. The walls were pale yellow and there were a lot of live plants. The wonderful aromas rising from the steam tables reminded me I hadn't had dinner.

I chose lasagna and a green salad; Sandy got the same, plus a huge oatmeal-raisin cookie. Danny chose the Mexican combination plate.

We settled ourselves at a round table and concentrated on eating for a few minutes. Then I asked, "So what happened, Danny?"

He popped a tortilla chip into his mouth, crunched and swallowed it before answering. "Paul and Red buddied up for the last dive. It was Red's third, Paul's second. Red had gotten a couple of lobsters on his other dives. Paul hadn't gotten any. He'd been skunked on the previous Wednesday Warriors trip and was determined to get at least one on this dive.

"As you know, Paul and Red have been diving together for decades. They always decide on depth and time limits before they enter the water. In the past, they terminated dives when conditions changed for the worst. That happened today. When they jumped in, the water was clear and flat. Not long after, the visibility deteriorated and a current came up.

"Red signaled up but Paul said 'no.' He wanted to finish the dive. Unfortunately, when it was time to ascend, they couldn't find the anchorline. In searching for it, Red exceeded his no decompression time and Paul became exhausted. The current was so strong he couldn't hold onto the line so he aborted his safety stop and went right to the surface. Red was worried about Paul and didn't make his stop either. He might not have gotten bent if he had.

"On the surface, Paul struggled to swim against the current. Red stayed nearby and both of them were rapidly carried away from the current line and the boat. Red noticed Paul hadn't inflated his BCD and yelled at him to do so. Instead, Paul spit out his regulator and sank like a stone. It happened in a split second. Later, he said he couldn't breathe and thought his tank was empty.

"When Red saw Paul go under, he went after him.

"The divemaster and I were already in the *California Diver*'s dinghy and we headed out to them.

"By the time we got there, Red had grabbed Paul and was about to surface. Paul was coughing and gasping for breath.

"It took all three of us to get Paul into the dinghy. He's a big man. When we got to the boat, the crew hauled him up on deck and put an oxygen mask on him. He was chilled to the bone. Since he couldn't remove his wetsuit on his own we cut it off and wrapped him in several blankets.

"We'd just finished doing that when Red took me aside. He had a lot of pain in his left shoulder and thought he might be bent. We put an oxygen mask on him. We helped him get out of his drysuit and wrapped him in blankets."

Danny stopped for a minute and took a drink of his Coke. I realized I was holding my breath. I exhaled and tried to breathe normally. Sandy was very pale and still. Danny resumed his story.

"The Coast Guard 'copter arrived about 40 minutes later. Not long after that, Paul and Red were on their way here for treatment."

Cathy joined us at the table.

"How's Paul," I asked.

"He's asleep now," Cathy said. She looked tired but relieved. "The doctors say he is suffering from exhaustion and near drowning, not a heart attack. He should make a full recovery.

"I don't think he'll ever forgive himself for getting Red bent, however. He feels just terrible about that.

"How is Red?"

"Also doing well," Sandy said. "The doctor says he should be fine." Her voice broke as she spoke and tears welled up in her eyes. She leaned over to hug Cathy and the two women clung to each other for a few minutes. I had to blow my nose, too.

We visited Dad again before leaving the hospital; then I went home with Danny. Sandy and Cathy would wait for Dad to get out of the chamber, which wouldn't be long, and drive home with him in my truck.

Several miles passed without words, though Danny reached for my hand as soon as we were up to speed on the freeway. The emotional connection between us was tangible.

"We were lucky today, Cinnamon," he said. "We came close to losing two divers. I was really scared. When Paul spit out his regulator and sank I thought he was a dead man. And when it looked as if he would survive, we discovered Red was bent. I kept waiting for another shoe to drop."

"But they're okay," I said. "It's all going to be okay." I squeezed his hand and he looked at me, his face showing the strain of the day.

"I'll never forget this," he said. "Not if I live to be 120."

Chapter 39

I spent the night at Danny's. We fell asleep nestled together like two spoons, taking comfort in being close. In the morning, Danny dropped me at my place so I could change my clothes.

Before I left for Greene's, I listened to the voice mail messages on my landline and cell. There were dozens from people concerned about Dad. Way too many to return. I'd have to post a note about his accident and recovery on our website.

Then there was this message: "Hi Cinnamon. This is Kimberly. Call me back."

She didn't leave a number and the only thing that showed up on my cell was "Anonymous."

At Greene's, I told the staff what had happened to Dad and Paul and we rescheduled people to cover Dad's job for the next few days. I added the note about yesterday's events to the website and settled down to business.

Surprise, surprise, Dad showed up just before noon, insisting he was a little tired but perfectly able to work. We tried to talk him out of it but he was adamant.

"There's absolutely nothing wrong with my mind," he informed us. "And I'm still the boss here."

So that was that. And besides, someone needed to talk to all of the people who were calling and stopping by to find out how he was. News of his and Paul's accidents had spread like wildfire through Cliffview.

In the midst of the chaos, Larry Walker phoned.

"Are we still on for this evening?" he asked.

For a few minutes, I couldn't remember who the hell Larry Walker was. Then it hit me. He was the only one of Tom's fraternity brothers who had responded to the e-mails I'd sent. I thought about canceling, then reconsidered.

"Sure."

"Great," he replied. "I've been looking through my yearbooks and pictures to refresh my memory. I know you'll want to see them."

"Absolutely."

The rest of the day passed in a blur of activity. I stopped at McDonald's on my way out of town and picked up a Big Mac, fries and a Diet Coke. I ate as I made the scenic drive south to Santa Monica along the Pacific Coast Highway.

Walker lived in a luxury apartment building on Ocean Park Boulevard. My GPS delivered me right to the building's front door. After an inquisition by the parking attendant, I left my truck in the subterranean garage and took an elevator to the lobby, where the concierge called Larry. He said, "Mr. Walker will meet you when you get off the elevator on the 10th floor."

The man standing in the hall when the doors opened was tall, with a healthy head of stylishly cut blond hair. His dark blue eyes looked sincere behind a pair of rimless glasses. He wore khaki slacks and a navy blue polo shirt.

"Cinnamon," he greeted me, shaking my hand enthusiastically, "great to meet you."

Larry's apartment offered a beautiful view of the bay. To the south, there was Venice's Pacific Park, with its solar powered Ferris wheel and rollercoaster. To the north, moving streams of white and red lights defined PCH as cars wound their way up and down the coast.

The apartment was spacious and comfortably furnished. Besides the living room, there was a small kitchen, a nice dining area and two closed doors, which I assumed led to bedrooms.

I'd thought a lot about which questions might elicit the information I wanted but I never got to ask them. Larry was a true salesman, outgoing and talkative. He showed me around his suite and offered refreshments. He'd picked up a cheese, cracker and vegetable platter from a nearby deli and set it on the coffee table. He fixed himself a scotch/soda and seemed disappointed that all I wanted was a glass of water.

From the time we met in the hall, he talked nonstop. Eventually, we were seated on the sofa. Next to the snack platter were four UCLA yearbooks. After consuming several crackers, a couple of carrots and a stick of celery, Larry picked up one of the books.

"Many fond memories from those years," he said. "The golden days of my youth."

I'd noticed that all of the yearbooks had yellow notes marking certain pages. Larry opened the book he held to one of them and pointed to a photo of the tennis team, of which he had been a member. In another photo on the same page he was holding a trophy. The youthful Larry was tanned, trim and gorgeous, with a megawatt smile. The middle aged Larry next to me was still attractive, but judging by the lumpiness of his middle, hadn't been on a tennis court for many years.

"I was going to go pro," he told me, "till I blew out my knee skiing. My game was never the same after that."

Larry picked up a second book and flipped through it to a note on a page devoted to the ski team. There he was, aiming his lady killer smile at the camera and holding another trophy.

A third yellow note marked his fraternity's page. He handed me the book. As I perused a large photo of smiling young men and the list of names under it, Larry said: "You know at least three of these guys, don't you, Cinnamon?"

Busted. For a minute I was speechless. Honesty seemed the only recourse. "Yes I do. We were all in the Bahamas on a boat recently."

"Where Tom and Dave died."

"Yes."

"I looked you up on the internet. I know you work in your dad's camera store. You aren't writing a history of my fraternity, are you?"

"No. I'm trying to find out who murdered Tom and why Dave died. I didn't know if you'd talk to me if I told you that.

"Miami police officers are investigating the Bahamas deaths. If they are getting anywhere, however, they aren't saying. My boyfriend Danny ran that trip. We'd like to know what happened. I'd like Danny to know that whatever it was, it wasn't his fault."

"Dave and Laura are good friends," Walker told me. "I called her when I heard he had died and she told me what Mike had told her. He said he and Dave did not know Tom would be on the trip until he and Kimberly got on the airport shuttle bus. They briefly discussed cancelling the entire vacation and decided that would be a victory for Tom. So they went and, according to Mike, regretted it immediately.

"Unfortunately, Laura had some place to go and had to end our conversation before she could tell me more. I haven't had a chance to speak with her since then. I looked for info online and found a detailed newspaper article that even listed who was on the boat. Your unusual name caught my eye. Not long afterward, I got your e-mail."

I said: "Tom and Kimberly joined us at the last minute, when another couple dropped off because of a medical emergency. Danny was busy getting ready to leave and didn't have a chance to notify anyone.

"Dave and Mike weren't the only ones who were upset to see Tom, though they never told anyone. Tom's ex-girlfriend Jessica didn't know he was going either.

"She told me later that Tom asked her not to mention their past relationship. He said his wife would be jealous."

"I wouldn't spread this around," Larry cautioned. "Because I'm sure Mike wouldn't want old gossip circulating again."

"If it's critical information I'll have to tell the police," I pointed out.

Larry nodded. "I understand that.

"Mike and Dave were very close, they'd known each other since childhood and roomed together in our fraternity house. In our junior year, Tom called a special meeting and said we needed to get rid of the 'fags' in our fraternity. The 'fags' he wanted kicked out were Mike and Dave."

"Those kinds of allegations can be very damaging," I said.

Larry nodded. "You bet. Tom, however, misjudged us. Everyone liked Mike and Dave. We didn't know if they were gay and we didn't care. Mike was captain of our stellar baseball team and chapter president. Dave was our treasurer. Tom, on the other hand, was an arrogant SOB who alienated everyone he met. We regretted having made him a member.

"When we found out Tom and Mike were dating the same girl we figured Tom was simply trying to eliminate the competition."

"What happened?"

"We kicked Tom out. Mike married the girl a couple of years later."

"Barbara?"

"Yes."

Not much later, Larry rode down in the elevator with me.

"You've been very helpful," I said. "Sorry for the deception."

Larry chuckled. "I'm not. I had a wonderful time reliving my college days, Cinnamon. You were a great audience.

"Besides, I also want whoever is responsible for Dave's death caught. He was a great guy. Laura is heartbroken. If you need anything else, please feel free to call or e-mail me."

He handed me one of his business cards, we shook hands and I left.

On the drive home along the coast, I remembered Tom's muttered remark about "faggots" during that breakfast on the *DD II*. Given what had happened the first time he made that charge, it seemed insane he'd done it again. Hadn't he learned anything from the fraternity debacle? I recalled that remark had clearly bothered Dave while Mike had tried to ignore it. Would either of them have wanted to get rid of their tormentor so much that they would kill him?

Chapter 40

Dad had his last chamber treatment the next morning and came into work afterward. He looked and acted normal, which was good. We still had a way above average number of phone calls and drop-in visitors and they all wanted to talk to him.

"When they see me here, they'll know I'm okay," Dad predicted. "I'll be old news by tomorrow."

He was off by a couple of days that were so hectic I didn't have the time or the energy to wonder where Danny was and why he hadn't called.

The frantic pace peaked on Saturday. I had a kid birthday party to video at noon and a wedding to photograph in the late afternoon. Neither shoot went smoothly. The last one took longer than I expected. By the time I returned to the store to unload the van, everyone else was long gone.

When I finally arrived home I was so tired I took the elevator from the underground garage to the second floor instead of walking.

As I was unlocking my door I heard music. That was odd. Nothing that plays music should be on when I'm not there. I pushed the door open cautiously.

I couldn't believe my eyes. The condo was lit by more than a dozen candles. Danny was in the kitchen, his back to me, singing along with one of my Jimmy Buffett CDs. When he turned and saw me, he grinned and held up two lobsters.

"Hope you don't have dinner plans," he said.

"What the heck is going on?" I asked, wrapping my arms around Danny. A man in my kitchen cooking lobsters is a fantasy come true. Danny kissed the top of my head.

"I'll tell you all about it later. Slip into something comfortable, take a shower if you want, dinner will be ready in about 30 minutes."

After I showered and changed into workout pants and a long sleeved turtleneck, I sat at the breakfast bar, sipping an ice cold Corona and watching Danny cook. Sam, he told me, was sleeping over at a friend's house.

Danny is the world's worst barbecue chef and nearly everything he grills turns to charcoal. Luckily, lobsters are a different story. Not only is he a great lobster catcher, no one is better at cooking them than he is. While they steamed, he dumped a bag of mixed salad greens into a bowl and sliced tomato, avocado and radishes to add to it. He baked two potatoes in the microwave and melted butter for lobster dipping.

We didn't talk, just listened to the music as I relaxed and Danny worked.

He'd set the table and it, too, was candle lit. When the food was ready, Danny ushered me over to the table, pulling out my chair for me.

The meal was wonderful. I enjoyed every succulent bite of dipped-in-melted-butter lobster. The potatoes and salad were perfect complements.

While we ate, Danny and I discussed Paul and Dad's accidents. Dad, I told him was doing great.

"I know," Danny said. "I've spoken to him every day since he got bent."

That was a surprise. "You talked to him and not me?"

"You were always busy or off some place," Danny said. "You weren't home when I called Thursday night, either."

"Well," I said, "if you thought I was out with Tony, you were wrong."

Danny grinned. "I know you weren't with him, he was at Flanagan's with someone else."

"You went to Flanagan's without me?"

"Yes. As I said, I called but you didn't answer. I came by but you weren't home. So I went to Flanagan's by myself."

"Oh," I said, trying to sound casual. "Who did you say Tony was with?"

"I didn't say. But it was that cute little blond waitress from Paris restaurant."

I remembered that woman. The day we'd had lunch there, she'd flirted with Tony and totally ignored me. Now I knew why. Changing the subject, I said, "I had an interview on Thursday night with Larry Walker. He was in the same fraternity at UCLA as Tom, Dave and Mike. He lives in one of those big apartment buildings on Ocean Park Boulevard in Santa Monica."

Danny raised an eyebrow. "Learn anything?"

I told him what I'd found out from Larry, adding, "Kimberly's gone. I went by the Tiburon villa on Wednesday and it looks deserted. Her maiden name was Jensen and her mother lives in Santa Monica so I called about 50 Jensens and left messages asking her to call me. She did that when I was at Valley View. She didn't leave her number. I'll have to start over."

"I think she listed her mother as her emergency contact on the form for my Bahamas trip," Danny said. "I'll look it up and give you a call tomorrow."

Oh double shit. When Danny looked at those forms he'd know they were copies. I tried to brush back a lock of hair and managed to knock over my beer. Its contents ran over the edge of the table and spattered the floor.

Danny and I mopped up the mess with paper towels and a sponge. When we finished, we cleared the table, loaded the dishwasher and cleaned up the kitchen.

"I have a confession," I said, scrubbing away at the pot he'd steamed the lobsters in.

Danny looked apprehensive. "Does it have anything to do with Tony?"

"No. This is much worse. I took the Bahamas trip forms from your office while you were gone Wednesday. I replaced them with copies."

Danny absorbed that, looking puzzled. "Why?"

"Tony insisted I send the logbook and the scrap of paper we found to the Miami detectives. If they decided to fingerprint them, they'd need comparison prints. I thought they could get those off the forms."

"Why didn't you just ask me?"

"I was afraid you wouldn't give them to me. You've been acting weird since we got back from the Bahamas."

Danny took the pot from me and put it back in the soapy water. Then he wound his arms around me. "All you had to do was ask."

"You're not mad?"

"Yes and no. You should have asked. But I know why you didn't. I haven't been easy to get along with recently."

I rolled my eyes. "Now there's a revelation."

"Don't be a smart ass," Danny was quiet for a minute, just hugging me. Then he continued. "Sam is going back to his mom's. He'll only be here for another month, maybe less if the babies come early. I miss him already."

There was another pause. "You know I want to get married and have more kids. You're not ready. I've been trying to figure out if I should wait till you are. I think there's a chance you'll never be ready."

"What did you decide?" Now I was apprehensive.

"Not to wait."

I pushed him away. "You're breaking up with me?"

"No." He pulled me close. "But I was going to."

"What made you change your mind?"

"I love you, Sunshine. I'm absolutely miserable when you're not around."

"Oh." I didn't get to say anything more for a long time.

Later, as I was falling asleep, Danny said, "I also have a confession."

"What?"

"Kimberly Tiburon and Mike Keating are having an affair. Or at least they were on our Bahamas trip."

"What?" I bolted upright. "How do you know?"

"Remember the night I went up on deck to look at the comet? It was after a dive on the Sugar Wreck."

"No. Or rather, yes, I think I recall something like that."

"We came back from the dive," Danny explained. "Pete was complaining that Tom had ditched him underwater. You went below to our stateroom, I went up on the sundeck to look at the night sky. I was standing there when I heard noises coming from the dinghy. I went over and lifted up the cover."

"Mike and Kimberly were in there."

"Yes. I dropped the cover and got out of there in a hurry."

"Why didn't you tell me?"

"I was embarrassed as hell. They were naked. I should have realized all those noises meant they were having sex."

"They say anything to you?"

"Mike took me aside the next day and asked me not to tell anyone what I'd seen."

"I'm not just 'anyone.'"

"I know. But the longer I waited the harder it was. I knew you'd be pissed."

I opened my mouth to object, but Danny put an index finger against my lips.

"I promise not to keep secrets from you," he said, "if you promise not to steal from me."

Chapter 41

When I was growing up, Dad loved Jack Smith's humorous column in the Los Angeles Times so much that he read it out loud. Now deceased, Smith claimed those who said Southern California had no seasons were wrong, it did indeed have them: "You just didn't know what season it was going to be when you got up in the morning."

On Saturday it had been summer. On Sunday it was winter. There was a storm brewing off the coast and the sun didn't make an appearance all day. Danny and I went to The Bakery for breakfast, huddling next to a heat lamp at a table on the patio while consuming lattes, hard boiled eggs and whole wheat English muffins with strawberry jam. Most people had had the good sense to stay indoors and only one other table was occupied.

Afterward, I went to Greene's and Danny went to Cliffview Divers. He called later to give me the emergency number listed on Kimberly's Bahamas trip form. When I dialed it, a woman answered. I asked for Kimberly.

"She's not here right now, may I ask who's calling?"

I recited my name and number.

"Oh, Cinnamon. This is her mother. I know she wants to talk to you. I'll tell her you called."

After we had hung up I realized I hadn't asked when Kimberly was expected back.

It started to rain after lunch. People who have to deal with snow and ice consider rain a much lesser evil. In California, however it's a big deal. We get so little rain that oil accumulates on our roads and highways. When it rains, the water and oil make the streets slippery.

Tony called in the middle of the afternoon.

"Very bad crash on Hilltop Road. I'll pick you up in ten. Do you have rain gear?"

"An umbrella and boots."

"I'll bring some stuff for you."

By the time Tony showed up, the rain was coming down in torrents and a nasty wind had sprung up. When he opened the store's back door a blast of cold, wet air blew in. He was wearing a yellow rain slicker with a hood, yellow pants and black rubber boots. He'd brought a matching outfit for me. As near as I could tell, it was the same size as his. I dressed quickly, rolling up the legs and arms of the outfit, and we left in his car.

It was raining so heavily the windshield wipers could barely keep up. Tony turned on his lights and siren, driving slowly and carefully.

The crash covered both sides of Hilltop Road and spilled over onto one shoulder. Five cars were involved. One Cliffview PD car was already on the scene, two more, along with three ambulances and a tow truck, showed up minutes later.

"Two dead, nine injured," Tony told me. "We've asked for more tow trucks and ambulances but everybody's busy."

While the other crime scenes I'd worked had been fascinating this one was grim and disturbing. There were wounded, traumatized people everywhere. I'd never seen so much blood.

The rain was relentless. I'd put a special covering over the camera to protect it and Tony held an umbrella over me while I shot, but it was impossible to keep everything completely dry.

The last thing we did was photograph the dead, both teenagers. The bodies were covered with white plastic, which Tony and another officer held up for a few quick shots.

The expensive new sports car the boy had lost control of was now wrapped around a tree. He and his female passenger hadn't been wearing seatbelts. Both had been ejected and killed instantly.

Young lives wasted. It was unsettling. Parents and friends would be devastated.

It was still raining when we finished. We drove to Greene's and I invited Tony in for a cup of coffee. He parked behind the store and we used the back door. We took off our dripping rain gear in the hall, hanging it on pegs put there for that purpose. I was chilled to the bone. Tony's hands and face were red with cold.

I brewed fresh coffee and the two of us sat in my office sipping it, holding the warm mugs with both hands.

"That was a bad one," Tony said at last. "Hope it hasn't changed your mind about crime scene photography."

"It hasn't but I'm glad they're not all like that."

"We found out what happened to the Martins," Tony said. "They'd sent a letter to their lawyer. Unfortunately, he was out of town when their bodies were found. He called us when he got back.

"They planned their deaths. Mrs. Martin explained they were old and life had gotten too painful and difficult. Her husband had Alzheimer's and she wasn't going to be able to take care of him much longer. They were going to take sleeping pills, wash them down with Dom Pérignon, then sail off together in their dinghy to meet their maker.

"We found an empty bottle of sleeping pills in the dinghy. We didn't find the champagne.

"Unfortunately, things didn't go exactly as they planned. Ginnie apparently fell out of the little sailboat. Maybe she dropped the champagne bottle and tried to retrieve it. We know she tried to get back in, there were scratches on her lower arms and paint from the dinghy under her fingernails. Her system, however, was full of sleeping pills and champagne. Her struggle couldn't have lasted long. She drowned."

"How awful," I said. "Those poor people."

"The Martins made a new will two months ago," Tony continued. "They left their money to a library and a church and set up a trust fund for their cat."

"Wow. So their deaths aren't related to Tom's at all."

"That's correct," Tony said.

Chapter 42

Danny spent the night at my place. Things were really good between us at last. I had to think the baby boom we were experiencing, with both Sandy and Danny's ex-wife expecting, had increased his already strong nesting urge. Maybe spending time with my new brother, due in a few months, would change his mind. I'd lived with my best friend for a short time, right after her first baby was born. Dirty diapers, sleepless nights and loads of laundry were certainly not things I found appealing.

Kimberly called me after lunch. "What do you want, Cinnamon?" She sounded irritated.

"I came by a couple of days ago. The villa looks deserted."

"Yes. Well, I'm staying at my mom's for a while."

"Is the house for sale?"

"Not yet. Why? Do you know someone who's interested in it?"

"Could be," I lied.

"Exactly what do you want?"

"I have something to discuss with you."

"I'm listening."

"I'd rather do it in person."

"Oh for heaven's sake," Kimberly said. "I'm going to be in Beachland most of Wednesday. Come by about 3:00."

I looked forward to seeing her reaction when I asked about her affair with Mike Keating.

In late afternoon I went to Cliffview PD to download the images of Sunday's horrible auto accident. Tony wasn't in when I got there, and hadn't come in when I finished.

The next day I waited impatiently for my Beachland visit. Of course, I left too early and arrived about 15 minutes before I was expected. The gate was open and I drove right in. Mine was the only car in the circular driveway and the house was dark.

Little had changed since the last time I'd been there except the grounds looked even seedier. The grass was ankle high; the bushes and trees were reverting to their natural state.

The front door wasn't locked and I walked on in. A shaft of light from the open door illuminated the staircase leading to the second floor.

"Kimberly," I yelled, my voice echoing off the foyer's wood paneled walls and tile floor. "It's Cinnamon."

"Come on up," she yelled back. "Go to Tom's office." I couldn't tell exactly where her voice was coming from.

I closed the front door. Now it was totally dark. I felt along the wall until I found a light switch. It didn't work. I carry a tiny dive light in my purse. I dug it out and pushed a button. Using the beam to light the way, I climbed the wooden staircase, wondering what had happened to the electricity.

At the top of the stairs, I paused.

"Kimberly?" This disappearing act was getting old.

"Go to Tom's office," Kimberly said from somewhere, "I'll be there in a bit."

There was a faint glow ahead of me. I walked slowly down the hall toward it. When I turned the corner, I saw light spilling through the door of Tom's office. The window coverings, drawn elsewhere in the house, had been opened here. Kimberly appeared in the doorway a few minutes later. She carried two small bottles of water.

"This is all I have in the way of refreshments," she said, loosening the cap of one bottle and handing it to me.

She walked around Tom's desk and sat down in the chair behind it, opening her bottle and taking a long drink. I did the same.

"It's dangerous walking around in here," I complained. "Is the electricity turned off?"

"Yes, along with the gas and water. Utilities for this monstrosity cost a fortune."

"Why don't you sell it?" I drained my bottle.

"It's not mine to sell. Tom's affairs are a mess. I can't get any money from his estate for anything. I'm going to have to get a job." Kimberly's face wrinkled in distaste.

"Surely there's money for the villa's upkeep."

"You would think so. Yet I haven't been able to get a penny.

"By the way, someone told me you had Dave Pecot's logbook.

Where is it?"

"I offered it to Laura Pecot, who suggested I give it to Mike. He didn't want it either."

"What did you do with it?"

For some reason the question struck me as odd. "It's in a safe place," I said. "Why do you ask?"

"Just curious. Now, what is it you wanted?"

I went for the shock factor. "How long have you and Mike been lovers?" I asked.

That got a reaction. Kimberly was shuffling papers on Tom's desk. Her head jerked up and she stared at me.

"Where did you hear that?"

"Danny saw the two of you naked in the dinghy on the sundeck."

Kimberly waved her hand dismissively. "Mike was doing some legal work for me. Something I didn't want Tom to know about. We thought the dinghy would give us privacy. It was miserably hot in there so of course we wore as little as possible. I had on a bikini and Mike was wearing trunks so there was a lot of bare skin."

I found Kimberly's explanation ludicrous. "Danny said you were having sex."

"Danny has quite the imagination." There was a nasty edge to Kimberly's voice.

"What kind of legal work was Mike doing for you?"

"That's none of your business.

"Look. I'm not feeling well. You should leave. Try not to trip and fall down the stairs."

Wow. I was still struggling with the concept of a totally non-mousey Mouse as I started down the hall. When I turned the corner, the door to Tom's office slammed shut, eliminating the only source of light. It was pitch black. Suddenly, I felt disoriented and dizzy.

I found the little dive light in my purse, turned it on and walked slowly toward the staircase. I was having trouble with my balance and remained upright only because I kept one hand on the wall.

I'm not really sure what happened. The room began to spin and suddenly I was tumbling down the stairs. I dropped purse, the empty water bottle and the light, screaming and grasping frantically for something to break my fall. There was only thin air.

Thump, thump, thump, thump, thump. The last thing I remember was hitting my head on the tile floor at the bottom of the stairs.

Chapter 43

I don't know how long I was out. Awakening in a chilly room, I thought I was blind because I couldn't see anything. I felt as if I'd been run over by a truck. I struggled to sit up and groaned.

"Cinnamon, are you okay?" I didn't recognize the voice immediately.

"Who's there?"

"Mike, Mike Keating." He scooted closer and touched my arm.

"Where are we?"

"In the basement of Tom's house."

"Why?"

"Why else?" Mike sighed. "We know too much. Now Kimberly has to get rid of us."

"How did you get here?"

"Kimberly put something in the bottled water she gave me, something that made me dizzy. I passed out and came to here. You arrived in the dumbwaiter. I probably did, too."

"What is she going to do with us?"

"I don't know. But I doubt it will be pleasant."

"How long have you been here?"

"My watch and phone are gone. Kimberly must have taken them. But I got to the villa about noon. What time did you get here?"

"Just before three. Was I out long?"

"I don't think so. I've completely lost track of time, though.

"We're in the wine cellar. I've found bottles stacked in racks. Sampled a couple. I couldn't stand Tom but I have to admit, the asshole had exquisite taste in wine."

"Find any vents or doors?"

"One solid wood door, leading to the rest of the basement and one very solid metal door, leading to the outside. Both have deadbolt locks that require keys I can't find. If there are any vents they are higher than I can reach."

"How about the dumbwaiter?"

"It stopped working after it brought you down. She must have turned off the emergency generator."

"Do you have any painkillers? I fell down the stairs before I passed out."

"How about a really nice Merlot? It made me feel better. You'll have to drink it from the bottle, though, there isn't any crystal."

He handed me the bottle and I took a swallow.

"Is my purse here?"

"Oh yeah," I heard Mike moving slowly to my right, shuffling his feet. He was back in a couple of minutes with my purse.

"Don't bother looking for your phone, it's not in there."

That was disappointing. I did a thorough search anyway, finding the tiny dive light and a small container of aspirin. I opened the container and shook out two pills, popping them into my mouth and washing them down with the last of the wine.

I was surprised to find the light. I was sure I'd dropped it when I fell down the stairs. I turned it on and the little beam sliced through the darkness around us.

"Bless you."

We were in a long, narrow room. The walls were lined with wooden racks filled with bottles of wine. The floor was slate. Very chilly slate. I saw the two doors Mike had described and the shaft that housed the dumbwaiter. High above us were two vents, way too small for either of us to get through even if we could reach them.

I walked over to the door that led to the outside. It was, indeed, metal, with a double bolt lock and no key. The other door was also locked and keyless. I shuffled over to the dumbwaiter. There was a button on the front. Nothing happened when I pushed it.

I walked back to Mike and sat down, turning the light off.

"I don't want to use up the batteries."

We sat side by side in the dark for a few minutes.

"Do you have your Swiss army knife?"

"Yes. It's proven handy in removing wine bottle corks."

I tried to think of other uses for the knife. The headache began to subside and I felt better.

"Why did you come here today?" Mike asked.

"I wanted to talk to Kimberly about the affair you and she were having. She denied it."

Mike sighed. "Biggest mistake I've ever made."

"How did you get together?"

"Kimberly came to see me last summer. She wanted me to find a loophole in the prenuptial she'd signed. Otherwise, she'd only get a token sum if she divorced Tom or the proceeds of a relatively small life insurance policy if he died of natural causes while they were married."

"Had you met her before?"

"No."

"Didn't you think it was odd that the wife of a man who tried to get you kicked out of your college fraternity would come to you for help?"

I heard Mike shift positions on the cool floor. "How did you find out about that?"

"One of your fraternity brothers told me."

"Nobody has any secrets anymore," Mike said bitterly, then continued: "I worked a high profile divorce case last year and my name was in the newspapers numerous times. Kimberly said that's how she heard about me. She claimed surprise that Tom and I knew each other so well. Now I think she saw me as a way to get back at him."

"Did you find a loophole in the prenup?"

"No. Tom was a lawyer and he had a very good lawyer draft it. It was bulletproof."

"How did your affair with Kimberly start?"

"She told me Tom was abusing her and cried on my shoulder."

"She's quite the little actress," I said.

"Well, it didn't have to be Academy Award quality. I wanted to believe her. One thing led to another. Pretty soon we were in the sack together. I liked the idea of sleeping with Tom's wife. It was a revenge of sorts."

"You weren't in love with her?"

"You've got to be kidding."

"Did Dave know about you and Kimberly?"

"He was a smart guy, he figured it out."

"Danny told me about finding you and Kimberly in the dinghy."

"That really spooked me. She wanted us to meet again, on the night Tom disappeared. I said absolutely no."

"Do you know who killed Tom?"

Mike was quiet for a long time.

"If you don't tell me I am going to figure it out eventually. I've got all the pieces of the puzzle, I just have to put them together."

Mike didn't speak right away. Then he said, "Dave and I were in our stateroom that night, getting ready for bed. He was writing in his log. He couldn't remember the bottom time of our last dive. You know how he was. Other people might have guessed at the time but Dave had to know exactly what it was. He went up on deck to look at his dive computer. He was gone longer than he needed to be. When he returned he was agitated and white as a sheet.

"He told me he'd found Tom on the deck, working on his cameras. When Dave set his logbook down to look at his computer, Tom picked it up. He said, 'Your middle initial is wrong here, Pecot. It should be 'F' for Faggot.' He used a waterproof marker to change the 'I' to 'F' and tossed the book at Dave. It fell on the deck and slid off into the ocean.

"Dave was horribly upset and not just about losing the logbook. It nearly destroyed him when Tom accused us of being gay in college. Temple Crystal condemns homosexuality and Dave would have been excommunicated if church leaders believed the charges were true. His marriage to Laura would have been annulled.

"Dave said he was going to put a stop to the lies for once and for all." Mike paused and seemed to be collecting his thoughts.

"What did you think he was going to do?"

"I had no idea. Dave had never been in a fight in his life. He paced around for a while before leaving our cabin. I was afraid he'd get hurt. I went after him a few minutes later.

"Kimberly and Dave were just pushing Tom into the sea when I came on deck. Dave looked sick.

"Kimberly was hysterical. She said Tom got mad when she insisted he follow the captain's orders to stay out of the water. He tried to slap her but slipped and fell, hitting his head on a scuba tank. He died instantly. Dave showed up just then and Kimberly begged him to help her push Tom overboard. She said if he was found on the deck everybody would think she killed him. She was so insistent Dave couldn't think straight. They dragged the body to the gate and pushed it into the sea.

"Watching the body sink, Dave knew he'd made a big mistake."

"Did you think Tom's death was an accident?"

"Then, yes. Now I know he didn't hit his head, he was

strangled. Kimberly did the deed with the cord of one of the battery chargers."

"Did she kill Dave, too?"

"He committed suicide. He'd lost a lot of money day trading and covered his losses with Temple Crystal funds. He cooked the books to hide that. When he talked to Laura via ship's radio during our trip she mentioned there was going to be an audit. Dave dreaded facing her and his father-in-law when they found out what he'd done. On top of that, he was now an accessory to murder."

"How do you know all that?"

"Dave wrote me a letter. I found it when I was getting off the boat in Miami. He asked me to destroy it after I read it so I tore it up and flushed the pieces down the toilet."

"I think I found part of it."

Even in the dark, I could feel Mike's interest.

"Oh? What does it say?"

"It's just a fragment. The only words I could make out are 'blame me.'"

"Can't be from the note Dave wrote me then. If you've still got it, could I see it? By the way, what happened to Dave's logbook? I should have taken it when you offered it to me, Dave would have wanted me to have it."

There was a lot of interest in a book nobody had wanted initially. "A cop friend of mine insisted I send the log and the note to the Miami police, so I did. I'll tell them you'd like to have when they're finished with it."

I had a sudden flash of inspiration. "Was it you or Kimberly who broke into my condo looking for the log?"

"Wasn't me," Mike said. "Must have been Kimberly."

Chapter 44

When Mike described straight-arrow Dave as a day-trading embezzler, his credibility took a nosedive. I found that charge preposterous. I also doubted Dave could have been persuaded to push a dead man overboard. He struck me as the kind of guy who would have reasoned with Kimberly, discussing the pros and cons of doing it until someone happened upon them and the point was moot or she got so irritated she did it herself.

As for who tossed Danny's and my places, Mike's answer to that question also rang false.

I started to voice my objections, then thought better of it. Why was Mike spinning these outrageous lies? Goosebumps popped up on my arms. I didn't want to think about that while I was alone in the dark with him. Better to wait till there were a lot of other people around. Right now I was feeling downright claustrophobic in that chilly wine cellar.

I had an idea. "Maybe we can climb up the inside of the dumbwaiter to the first floor," I said. "Loan me your knife."

Mike put his knife in my hand and the two of us made our way to the dumbwaiter in the dark. I turned on my little light and opened the dumbwaiter door. The metal box that went up and down delivering bottles of wine and bodies was roughly three by three feet and four feet high. It was level with the floor so carts could be wheeled in and out of it.

The dumbwaiter looked to be a rather recent addition. The shaft was enclosed with wallboard. I opened the blade of the knife and went to work on an edge. Within a few minutes, I had a small hole. A little later, Mike helped me pulled off an entire section, leaving a space more than large enough for us to squeeze through.

"Can you hand me my purse?"

Mike thrust the purse at me and I hung the strap over my head and one shoulder before climbing on top of the metal car. Once there, I used the light to look around.

"The door is level with my eyes and we're in luck, there's a handle," I told Mike. "You're a lot taller. I think you could climb out pretty easily."

Mike joined me atop the dumbwaiter car. The two of us now occupied a space smaller than the average shower. I was busy congratulating myself on my ingenuity when Mike opened the door to the first floor and dense smoke poured in.

"Holy hell! The house is on fire. We've got to get out of here," he said.

He crawled out onto the tile floor of a hot, dark, smoky room, then grabbed my hands and pulled me out. We were in the kitchen.

I saw a door to the outside on one wall.

"There's no key for the door," Mike said. "We'll have to get out here."

He had climbed up on a counter that had three French windows over it.

"Cinnamon! Come quick."

I was there in seconds. Night had fallen while we were in the wine cellar. Mike opened the window and cool, fresh air rushed in. He kicked out the screen and scrambled over the sill with me right behind him.

We raced toward the front of the house. We hadn't gotten far when a couple of windows blew out on the second floor, belching broken glass, smoke and fire. The heat was intense.

I have never been so scared in my life. My feet grew wings. We reached my truck and scrambled inside it as I fumbled for the keys in my purse. Not finding them, I dumped the contents on the floor at Mike's feet. There they were.

I started the truck, put it in gear and stepped on the gas, turning on the headlights while driving hell-bent toward the gate down the winding lane. As we took off, more windows in the house exploded. Orange-red flames filled the rearview mirror.

The gate at the end of the lane was closed. Who had done that or why I had no idea. While I knew there had to be a way to open it manually, I didn't know what that was. We stumbled out of the truck and stared at the wrought iron fence. About ten feet tall, it was capped with spikes. While we were in no danger from the fire here, we were both eager to be on the other side of that fence.

"We'll have to climb on top of the truck," I said, "I'll move it closer."

I drove the truck up against the fence, shearing off the passenger side rear view mirror and doing major damage to the body. I was so terrified my hands were shaking. We crawled up on the hood of the truck and then onto its roof.

Those little pointy spikes on the top of the fence were a real hazard but, adrenaline driven, I got over them somehow. Wearing only a long sleeved T-shirt and jeans, I was streamlined. I slid down the bars on other side and dropped to the ground.

Mike didn't make it over as easily. He was wearing a navy blue jacket, the front of which was unzipped. An inside shoulder of the jacket got caught on a spike. When he tried to slide down the bars, the weight of his body made freeing the jacket impossible.

Somehow Mike shrugged out of the jacket and slid down the fence, landing next to me with a thud.

He stumbled upright and looked at the jacket above him.

Just then a fire engine arrived and I realized I'd been hearing sirens for a while. A small crowd had formed across the street.

Mike stood at the bottom of the fence and jumped several times, trying to reach the jacket, which remained a few feet above his hands.

"Step on my hands," he ordered. "I'll lift you up and you can grab it."

I was watching two more fire engines and a police car arrive. The noise of their sirens was mind numbing and the flashing lights were blinding.

"Step on my hands, Cinnamon," Mike demanded. "Now."

"You by the fence. Get the hell out of there," a fireman yelled.

I turned and ran toward the street.

"Hold it right there," someone ordered. "Hands above your heads."

As Mike and I raised our hands, something on his wrist caught the light. Why had he told me he didn't have a watch?

Chapter 45

"It's Cinnamon Greene, Chief," I said, "And this is Mike Keating. We'll go quietly, we don't have any weapons."

"Cinnamon?" came the incredulous response. "What on earth are you doing here?" Chief Lawson stood in front of us with Tony by his side.

"I might ask you the same question," I said.

"We were told a house was on fire and the possible arsonists were trying to climb over the fence. Was that you and your friend here?"

"Yes," I said. "That's my truck over there, inside the fence. But we didn't set the fire."

"Let's go on down to the station," Lawson said, "See if we can sort this out."

"Okay," I sighed.

Mike and I got in the back seat of the black and white, Lawson and Tony got in the front.

"What are you doing here?" I asked. "I thought Beachland was in Santa Barbara PD's jurisdiction."

"The city has had a contract with us for the past five years," Lawson informed me.

Fifteen minutes later, we were at the police station, which contains a three person jail. Lawson decided to interview Mike, leaving me to Tony.

Before we started, Tony microwaved one of the jail's frozen dinners, usually reserved for inmates, and brought me a cup of coffee from the break room. I glanced at him as I was devouring a forkful of hash browns. The concern on his face was quickly replaced by an impersonal mask when our eyes met.

Tony videotaped our session. When I got to the part about

falling down the stairs and ending up in the wine cellar, he halted the taping so I could give a urine sample for testing. There's a 24 hour urgent care center across the street from the police station. We walked there and he waited while I submitted my sample. He suggested I have the doctor take a look at my bumps, bruises and scratches, but I declined. We returned to the station.

It was late when I finished my tale. I was exhausted and ached all over. I didn't know where Mike was and didn't care. I only wanted to go home to bed.

I had contacted Dad and Danny when I got to the station. Now Tony drove me to Danny's. He walked me to the door and waited until Danny opened the door.

"You look terrible," he said. "Shouldn't I take you to the emergency room?"

"We've been there already," Tony said. "She wouldn't let the doctor touch her. She says she's fine."

"All I need is a hot shower and good night's sleep."

"We were really worried about you. Nobody knew where you were," Danny said.

"Guess I forgot to tell anyone I was going to see Kimberly."

Not long after Tony left, I climbed into bed next to a wide awake Danny. I didn't think I'd be able to tell my story again that night but the coffee and a shower had given me a second wind. At the end, when I was telling Danny how Mike and I had climbed over the fence, I remembered Mike's reluctance to leave his jacket.

"It's not like he couldn't get another one. It's from a catalogue company. Dad has one just like it."

"Maybe it's not the jacket but what's in it," Danny pointed out. "Something in a pocket."

When that thought percolated through my brain I got out of bed and started pulling on my clothes. "Come on Danny. We've got to go get that jacket."

"Haven't you had enough for one day? Call Lawson, let him handle it."

"If we don't hurry, the jacket will be gone. If you won't come with me, I'm going alone. Where are your keys?"

A few minutes later, we were on our way to the Tiburon villa. The fire was out and the gate was closed when we got there. Clouds hid the moon and it was pitch dark. The acrid smell left by the fire was overpowering.

After parking his truck at the curb, Danny grabbed a heavy-duty light from the glove compartment and we walked over to the fence. Close up, we could see the damage to my truck was extensive.

"Holy shit," Danny said, playing the light long the truck's side. "You really did a number on it, didn't you?"

I was more concerned about the jacket. "It's still there, Danny. Can you lift me up?"

Danny set his light down and made a step with his hands. As I held onto the bars, he hefted me skyward. But the jacket remained just beyond my grasp.

"I need to climb onto your shoulders."

In the dark, this was harder than I expected. I grabbed a sleeve of the jacket and after repeated tries, was able to get it off the spike. I slid down the bars to the ground with it over my shoulder.

"Thanks a bunch. I was wondering how I'd reach that," said a voice next to us. "Thank you."

We'd been intent on our task and hadn't heard Mike's stealthy approach. He grabbed the jacket.

"Not so fast," Danny said, jerking the jacket out of Mike's hands. "Why is this is so important?"

"It's got sentimental value, that's all," Mike said. "Dave gave it to me. He's not around to give me another one. Please let me have it."

"Sorry," I said. "It's evidence in a crime. I'll be handing it over to the police."

I picked up Danny's light as Mike lunged for the jacket. Danny swung it out of his reach. Several items flew out of it and I heard them fall to the ground nearby.

The overgrown lawn complicated our search for the jacket's contents. I handed Danny his light and Mike turned on his. The three of us began to examine the ground around us. When a cell phone appeared in the bright beams, Mike pronounced it his and pounced on it. Mine showed up a few minutes later and I stuck it in a pocket.

"You told me you didn't have a cell phone, that Kimberly had taken it. You said she had mine, too," I said.

"I'd been drugged, I was still woozy."

"Is that why you also forgot you were wearing a watch?"

"I told you, I wasn't thinking clearly. I was still feeling the effects of whatever drug Kimberly put in our water."

"Then you won't mind if we look through the jacket pockets,"

Danny said.

"Have at it," Too late, I saw Mike swing something dark at Danny's head. He missed, hitting Danny's shoulder instead. In the scuffle that followed, Danny's light fell to the ground. I reached for it as the guys crashed into me. We all went down.

Mike got to his feet first. A shot rang out. Halfway up, Danny yelped and dropped to the ground. A second shot was fired. Legs rubbery with fear, I scrambled upright and bolted into the night. The gun fired twice more. My foot caught on something and I fell, rolling under some bushes.

There were no more shots. I looked back. Someone had picked up both lights and was searching the ground where Danny and I had been just minutes earlier. The fast, jerky way the lights were moving told me the holder was agitated. It must be Mike. I held my breath, expecting to see Danny's bloody body in the beam.

No body appeared. I hoped Danny had gotten away.

Mike found the jacket, picked it up and, after turning one light off, continued searching.

The remaining light moved erratically, shining here and there. I didn't know what to do. While Danny's truck wasn't far away he had the keys. Parked across the street was a black or dark blue SUV, which must be Mike's. Now I realized it had been there when I arrived at the mansion for the first time that afternoon.

When I saw a furtive movement near the SUV, I knew it had to be Danny. Crouching low, I ran for it, not sure what I'd do when I got there.

I found Danny pressed close to the rear bumper. He motioned me to go to the other side of the SUV but I shook my head and stayed where I was.

We watched the light sweep up and down along the fence. After Mike picked up two more items he turned it off.

When our eyes adjusted to the dark we saw a shadowy figure creeping cautiously our way. Danny waited until Mike got near the car before tackling him. Hard. The two of them fell to the ground and began scuffling. The gun went off one more time as a police car roared to a stop behind us, siren blasting and lights blazing.

Chapter 46

Chief Lawson and Tony erupted from the first car. Two more patrol cars arrived a few minutes later. Mike tried to get to his feet but Tony quickly put a knee was on his back and handcuffed him. Lawson handcuffed Danny, despite my protests.

"We'll get to the bottom of this at the station," he advised me. "Keep quiet or I'll handcuff you, too, Cinnamon."

So for the second time that night, Mike and I were hauled off to the police station. This time Danny came, too.

Before we left the mansion I said, "Are you okay Danny? Did he shoot you?"

"No," he said. "I wanted him to think he had, though. He's a terrible shot. I don't think he could hit an elephant if he was sitting on top of it."

The adrenaline that had given me a second wind wore off during the ride to Cliffview. I leaned back against the seat of the patrol car and dozed off.

The rest of the evening and the wee hours of the morning passed in a haze. Not long after we got there, Lawson and Tony handed us off to officers I didn't know and went home. My hands were tested for gunshot residue. I videotaped another statement and hoped it made sense. I answered question after question. I was alone in a room for what seemed forever.

Released at long last, I found Danny in the lobby, waiting for me. I smelled coffee. I led him down the hall to the break room, where we helped ourselves to doughnuts and coffee. I put a couple of dollars in the donations jar sitting next to the doughnut box just before Lawson appeared.

"Why are you still here?" he asked. "And why are you eating my doughnuts?"

"Don't worry, Chief, we left a couple for you and fed the kitty. Did you let Mike go?"

"Not yet. Mr. Keating gets to enjoy our hospitality awhile longer." Lawson grinned and rubbed his hands together.

"Did he admit he shot at us?" I asked.

"He claimed Danny shot at him," Lawson said, "but the gun is registered to his wife and he was the only one with gunshot residue on his hands."

"Did you find out what was in the jacket pockets?' I asked.

"Yep," Lawson said. "A ring that holds keys to the mansion and a Rohypnol pack with four empty bubbles."

"The water Kimberly gave me was drugged," I said. "That's why I passed out and fell down the stairs. But Mike was in the wine cellar when that happened."

"That's what he told you," Lawson said. "You don't know if it's true."

I mulled that over. "How did you get to the villa so fast?"

"We were already on our way. After you and Mike left, Tony and I reviewed your statements. You told us Mike didn't want to leave without his jacket. Mike, however, didn't mention it. We wondered why. We decided we'd better grab the jacket before someone else did. When heard shots, we called for backup.

"By the way, I called the Reverend Crystal a few minutes ago. I told him Mike claimed Dave Pecot had committed suicide because he'd stolen money from Temple Crystal to cover his day trading losses. The Rev. Crystal denies that. Emphatically. He says Pecot was like a son to him. A wonderful husband and a conscientious, hard working employee of the highest moral character. Taking money that didn't belong to him just wasn't something he would do. The Reverend offered to give forensic accountants unlimited access to Pecot's computers and the Temple's books, said if we found evidence of day trading or embezzlement he'd kiss my ass."

Chapter 47

A deputy had driven Danny's truck to the police station the night before but mine was still at the villa. Lawson said it had to be photographed and examined for forensic evidence before I got it back.

Danny dropped me off at Greene's. I wanted to talk to Dad before the store opened. He knew I had been at the police station — again — but didn't know why. I had just finished telling him and our staff what had taken place when the first phone call triggered by the Cliffview rumor mill came in. We spent the day dealing with an onslaught of calls, e-mails and visits from curious town folk.

Late that afternoon, Tony called. "We're finished with your truck. I don't think you'll be able to drive it though. There's been major damage. I'm going back to the mansion in a little while, if you want to meet a tow truck there I can give you a lift."

He picked me up about an hour later.

It was *deja vu* driving to Beachland for the third time in 24 hours. So much had happened. Shrouded in fog in the light of day, one side of the mansion looked like a scene from *Rebecca*. The other side looked normal. It gave me the creeps. Water puddled on the driveway and grounds. That distinctive burned smell was acute.

Tony had explained that my involvement in the case meant I would not be taking forensic photos of the mansion for CPD. That would be done by a detective from the Forensics Unit of the Santa Barbara County Sheriff's Department.

Said detective was waiting for Tony by the villa's open gate. I had learned that a neighbor closed the gate whenever she found it open to "Keep out the riffraff." We all inspected my truck. Tony was right, it was not drivable. I removed the CPD's photo equipment from the security box and, as Tony and the detective walked up the drive to the house, called the Cliffview Body Shop. Then I climbed into my vehicle to wait for the tow truck. I must have dozed off because the next thing I knew, there was a hand on my shoulder and Tony was asking:

"Who was in the house besides you and Mike?"

"Kimberly," I said, "Why?"

"We found a body."

"Male or female?"

"We're not sure. A deputy coroner is on his way here."

"Can I see it?" I asked.

"Maybe. A coroner's deputy needs to examine it first," Tony said.

The tow truck showed up and carted my vehicle off. I sat with Tony in his car while we awaited the deputy. He was busy writing a report on the unit's laptop. It was warm in there and I dozed off again. When I awakened, I spotted Tony talking to several people I didn't recognize. When he came back to the car he said, "Let's go see the body."

We walked to the house and Tony led the way to a room I recognized as Jefferson Tiburon's study. The villa was in better shape than I expected. While there was extensive smoke and water damage, the fire seemed to have been confined to a couple rooms on the second floor and those just below them on the first, one of which was the study.

"Over here," Tony said, indicating a pile of debris. "Follow in my footsteps."

I have to admit, I was dreading the sight of another corpse but at least this time there was no blood. Lying near the middle of a room was a charred lump, nearly unrecognizable as human. I shuddered. What a horrible way to die.

The coroner carefully turned the body over on its back. The face was blackened and didn't look like anyone I knew or had ever known. What remained of the hair was blond and the sparse clothing remnants had once been blue pants, a navy shirt and a navy scarf.

"Oh shit. It's Kimberly. I can't believe she didn't get out of the house. Where did the fire start? Was it arson?"

"What do you think?" Tony asked.

I looked around. "The fire started in Tom's office, which is right over this room. It's the most badly burned part of the house. Kimberly's body ended up here when the floor of the office collapsed."

Before we left the mansion, Tony led me around to the side of the house that was relatively unscathed, pointed to a metal door and said, "A key found in Mike's jacket opens this."

"What? That's the door to the wine cellar. That doesn't make sense. Why would Mike stay in a burning building when he could get out?"

"I have no idea," Tony admitted.

Back in Cliffview, Tony dropped me at my condo, where I flopped down on my bed. While I only intended to rest for a minute, I fell asleep almost instantly. My dreams were filled with fire, smoke and charcoal briquette bodies.

Chapter 48

Days passed. Life returned to near normal. My relationship with Danny was once again very good. At odd moments every now and then, however, I wondered if rough times were a thing of the past or lurking just below the surface.

Most nights I slept well. Not always, though. Just before a date with Danny after one particularly hectic day, I showered and lay down for a few minutes, drifting into a dream I'd had several times since the villa burned. I was snorkeling in the Bahamas and the *Dolphin Diver II* was engulfed in flames behind me. Suddenly I spied Dave's logbook lying on the bottom of the ocean. As I dived down to get it, Mike came out of nowhere and grabbed it. He shot to the surface holding it and laughing insanely.

The doorbell rang.

"It's only me," Danny said when I'd stumbled to the living room and demanded to know who was there. "Ready for dinner?"

I opened the door and stepped into his arms, putting my head on his chest. Danny drew me near. Warm and secure, I snuggled closer.

Danny kissed the top of my head. "That must have been one bad ass nightmare," he said, his mouth next to my ear.

I didn't want to let go of him but we were standing in the hall. I pulled him inside my condo and closed the door. A few minutes later, we went into the kitchen, where I poured two glasses of wine. We sipped it sitting side by side at the breakfast bar as I relived my dream.

In the telling, inspiration struck. "Getting out of the wine cellar was horrendous. I forgot that while I was at the mansion, both Kimberly and Mike asked me what I'd done with Dave's logbook."

"When you tried to give it to Mike, he wouldn't take it."

"True. I think he was shocked to see it. He'd thrown it

overboard and thought it was gone forever. Later, he began to wonder if there was something incriminating in it. Do you remember Mike's pet name for his wife?"

"Burgie. He said she was really good at breaking into...." Danny stopped and comprehension flooded his face

"Into her house," I finished. "She's probably equally good at breaking into other people's houses. Yours and mine, for instance."

"Looking for the logbook?" Danny asked.

"Exactly. She and Mike didn't find it because I left it in your shop with my photo gear after the Wednesday Warriors trip."

"Bet that's why Mike and I ended up in the wine cellar. He wanted to know what I'd done with the log. I should call Tony and tell him."

Danny made a face. "Can it wait till tomorrow? I'm hungry."

I was, too. We decided to walk to town instead of driving.

"Pizza?" I suggested as we started down the stairs.

"Let's save that for Sam. I was thinking of Sushi Sue's."

"Speaking of Sam, where is he?"

"With the babysitter," Danny said. "He has such a crush on Sara he practically pushed me out the door."

Danny wrapped an arm around my shoulder and I put an arm around his waist. When we reached the bottom of the stairs, we ran smack into Tony.

Even in the pale light supplied by Cliffview's old-fashioned streetlights, I could see he was clean-shaven. He wore civilian clothes and looked as if were ready for a date, a fact, I realized, not lost on Danny.

"Tony," I said. "This is serendipity. We've got things to tell you."

"I've got things to tell you, too. But I don't want to intrude on your date."

"We're just going to dinner at Sushi Sue's. Why don't you join us?"

"Or, we could come to the station tomorrow," Danny offered, tightening his grip on my shoulders.

Danny had issued a challenge. Tony decided to take it.

"I haven't had dinner," he said, "and I love sushi."

So the three of us walked through Cliffview's quiet streets together; me in the middle, with one of Danny's arms wrapped proprietarily around my shoulders and Tony on my other side, hands in his pockets. The air was still, without even a breath of sea breeze, which is unusual. A heavy dew had fallen and water beaded every exposed surface.

As we walked, I told Tony what Danny and I had been discussing before he arrived.

Sushi Sue's is very popular and we were lucky to get a table. We ordered three Japanese beers and several dishes to share.

"What did you want to tell us?" I asked Tony.

"Two Miami-Dade detectives arrived here a couple of days ago. The three of us conducted extensive interviews with Keating and his wife and searched their residence. You were right on the money about who burglarized your places. It was Mike and Barbara and they were looking for Dave's logbook. In a closet we found two blue jumpsuits with phony air conditioning company logos on them. The Keatings wore them to a Halloween party a few years back, calling themselves 'the coolest couple.'

"But that's not all. A thumbprint I found in your condo after it was tossed was left by Mike.

"Although Mike has admitted he strangled Tom he says he was temporarily insane when he did it.

"He claims Tom's accusations that he and Dave were gay were the trigger. He believed Tom would make them over and over on the trip, just as he had in college. Mike dreaded going through that again. When he learned Tom had changed the initial on Dave's treasured logbook and it ended up in the ocean he snapped. He went up on deck to confront Tom. The next thing he knew, Tom was dead and Kimberly was helping him push the body into the sea.

"This account is collaborated by the suicide note Dave wrote."

"What note?" Danny and I asked in unison.

"The one you found part of."

The 'blame me' paper? Only two words were legible," I pointed out.

"They were more pieces," Tony said.

"When he was away, Dave would write a letter to Laura every day. If he couldn't send them during the trip she would read them when he got home. Dave didn't care if Mike found those but he didn't want him to find the last one, which was written on a blank logbook page he had cut out and hidden in his carryon. Before he walked into the freezer and shut the door, he packed all of his things so his luggage was ready to go. He expected Laura to find the letter, hidden in a secret place where he usually kept money, when she unpacked.

"Mike found the letter by accident when he tried to stuff something into Dave's carryon because his was full.

"The taxis were waiting and Mike was in a hurry. He tore the letter into pieces and threw them in the toilet in his and Dave's cabin. He didn't check to see if all the pieces went down when he flushed and most of them didn't. The log's paper was waterproof and instead of sinking it floated. The police retrieved the pieces during their first search of the *DD II*. The scrap you sent them was very helpful.

"Dave's letter said Mike was so upset about what Tom had done to the logbook and his renewed accusations that he went up on deck to confront him.

"Dave wrote: 'Mike was very angry. I begged him to drop the matter. When he headed up there anyway, I knew I should go with him. If I had, Tom would still be alive. Blame me, it's my fault he's dead.'"

Tony continued. "Dave was a deeply religious man. He says he couldn't lie about what happened. If he told the truth, however, his life-long best friend would go to prison and might even be put to death. He couldn't live with that. He killed himself and asked Laura to destroy the letter. He thought he was saving Mike."

"Isn't suicide a sin?" This came from Danny.

"Temple Crystal members believe there are certain circumstances when it isn't," Tony said.

"What about fingerprints? Were any fingerprints found on the log and the paper scrap? Did the cops use the exemplars I sent?"

"Little Miss Detective," Tony said, smiling. "You never give up do you?"

"You got that right," Danny agreed.

I elbowed him in the ribs.

"The fingerprints on the fragment and the log weren't usable. The lab techs did use the forms you sent, however. They compared the handwriting on them to that on the letter fragments and concluded that Dave wrote them."

"How did he die?" I asked.

"Hypothermia. He froze to death."

"No drugs in his system?" I asked.

"No."

Tony wasn't finished. "If the dolphins hadn't brought Tom's body back to the boat we might never have known how he died.

"While it was unfortunate for Mike that the body was recovered, that also impacted Kimberly. With no body, she would have continued to get the monthly allowance Tom had arranged for her when they got married. That wouldn't stop until he was declared legally dead, which could have taken years. Since his body was found and it was obvious he didn't die from natural causes, the prenup kicked in and she was left penniless."

"How did Kimberly die?" I asked.

"Smoke inhalation," Tony said. "But her hands were bound with her scarf and her feet with an electrical cord.

"Can I tell you what I think?" I asked.

"Is there anyway to prevent that?" That was Danny's idea of a joke. He knew my opinion was forthcoming no matter what.

Tony said: "I'm very much interested in hearing your take."

"I believe Mike went the villa to kill Kimberly. She may have been making up her lost income by blackmailing him. He gave her two bottles of drugged water after he got there. I don't think he was expecting me. When I showed up he hid in another room.

"Kimberly had no inkling of his plans. To Mike's surprise, she gave me one of the bottles and we both drank them. I left the room just before she passed out. That's when he closed the door of the office, leaving me in the dark. A few minutes later, I passed out, too.

"Mike decided to make another attempt to find out what I'd done with the log. He sent me down to the wine cellar in the dumbwaiter before binding an unconscious Kimberly's hands and feet and starting a fire. He was in the wine cellar when I woke up. He didn't think we were in any danger from the fire because he had the mansion's keys in his jacket. I, however, figured out how to get out of the cellar and we didn't need a key.

"Mike must have been shocked when he opened the dumbwaiter door and discovered how quickly the fire had spread. "Still, he insisted we go out the window because he didn't want me to see him using a key to open the kitchen's outside door.

"We know he had Rohypnol tablets in his jacket pocket. He will probably claim, however, that Kimberly put them in his jacket when he was unconscious, and that the drug had been eliminated from his system by the time he was tested. Did the lab find that drug in my system, Mike's or Kimberly's?"

"Your body had traces of the drug," Tony said. "Mike's didn't. Kimberly's body was too badly burned to test. If your theory is correct, Mike probably thought her body would be too badly burned to establish a cause of death as well."

"Rohypnol. Isn't that one of the date rape drugs?" Danny asked.

"Yes," I said.

Danny's face clouded. "You said you were drugged but you never mentioned the name of the drug, Cinnamon."

Tony understood before I did. "The drug was used to make her lose consciousness, nothing else."

"Mike was busy binding Kimberly's hands and feet and setting a fire," I pointed out.

"How reassuring," Danny said. "You know, I don't think I'm ever going to have dinner with the two of you again. Can we talk about something other than mayhem and murder?"

"Good idea." Tony agreed instantly.

Still, we ate in silence for a while, struggling to come up with an acceptable dinner table topic. There were several false starts before the talk shifted to baseball. Danny and I are avid Dodgers fans. Turns out Tony is, too.

The three of us discussed team stats and next year's World Series possibilities while we finished our meal.

"My extended family goes to a lot of games," Tony said. "We have a suite and 'copter in to avoid the traffic. You'll have to come as my guests some time."

"I'd love that," I said. "I've never flown in a helicopter."

"Sounds great," Danny said with a notable lack of enthusiasm.

After dinner, we walked back to my place. In case Tony had forgotten who I was with, Danny linked one of his arms through mine.

"Has anyone checked out Mike's claims that Dave was a day trading embezzler?"

"Temple Crystal's books and Dave's financial affairs are being audited right now. We don't expect to find any evidence to support those claims."

We now stood in front of my building. "Want to come up? Have some coffee or something?"

Danny glared at Tony, soundlessly daring him to accept my offer.

Tony didn't accept that challenge. "Not tonight," he said, his eyes on mine. He looked tired. "It's been a long day. I'm on my way to Ojai. I've got tomorrow off."

"Have a good one," Danny said. I thought his words lacked sincerity. Holding my hand, he started up the stairs.

I dropped Danny's hand and turned to Tony, "Thanks for the update."

"No problem."

"Are you coming, Sunshine?" Danny asked impatiently.

"See you," I said to Tony, then turned and climbed the stairs toward Danny.

Acknowledgments

At the top of my wish list as a new diver was diving with dolphins. That happened three times before 1998. Two of those events were unexpected and involved a wild dolphin. One was a planned interaction with captive dolphins. While those were fun and memorable, none of them fulfilled my dream. That occurred during a week spent cruising White Sand Banks in the Bahamas where wild spotted dolphins have been swimming with snorkelers for more than three decades. The encounters happen at the dolphins' pleasure and last as long as they decide to stick around. The dolphins also control how close snorkelers come to them.

My magical wish-come-true-week was the basis for this book and the setting is real, though all of the people are fictional, as is the boat. The California town Cinnamon Greene and company live in is likewise fictional, as are all of the events you will read about.

For many years the only people who read my books were the agents to which they were submitted. When I decided I needed input and began asking people to read them and let me know what they thought, Joanne Cook, Joe Cook, Dave Finnern, Howard Hall, Dr. Jim Holm, Vicky Tasoff and Linda Whipple agreed. All of them came up with constructive comments, questions and suggestions. Some pointed out errors as well. I am grateful for their input. To say this is a better book because of them is an understatement!

About the Author

Bonnie J. Cardone grew up in Arizona, Chicago and Michigan. She moved to Southern California in 1967 and became a scuba diver in 1973. From then on, her goal was to dive as much of the world as possible.

In 1976 she was hired as an editor of Skin Diver, the world's largest and oldest diving magazine. The next 22 years were exciting and educational. The magazine and the sport grew far larger far faster than anyone expected. Meanwhile, Bonnie was writing hundreds of articles on almost every imaginable marine related subject and illustrating most of them with her photos.

When Bonnie was downsized in 1999, she did what she had always planned to do when she retired: she began writing mystery novels. She had already taken five UCLA extension writing classes and written several short mystery stories. At friend Gary Brandner's suggestion, she had joined Mystery Writers of America while she was a stay at home mom in the 1970s.

Bonnie became a member of Sisters in Crime in 1999 and, in 2000, became the editor of its national newsletter, a job that lasted nine years and provided a first class education in all aspects of the mystery field. During those years Bonnie attended two to three mystery conventions every year, meeting and photographing well-known mystery writers. She also attended author panels and interviews (and conducted a few of the latter for the newsletter).

At present, Bonnie is a freelancer who writes marine related articles for scuba diving publications and illustrates them with her photographs as well as writing mystery novels and short stories.

Photographs of a few of the marine creatures Cinnamon Greene and company might encounter while snorkeling and diving in California, the Bahamas and the Caribbean can be seen at www.bonniejcardone.com.

Praise for Murder Dives the Caribbean

"An intriguing mystery entangled with an enigma above and below the sea....A true compelling story that puts Bonnie J. Cardone in the first rank of mystery writers." —Clive Cussler, New York Times Best Selling author

"This is an easy to read novel with exciting turns of events that keep the reader engrossed to the end....no matter how hard one might try to second guess how Cinnamon will handle it, surprises are still likely to occur. Through all of Cinnamon's adventures, one can surely feel and recognize where she is almost to the point of even 'smelling the roses' of a Caribbean island." —Roger Roth

"I was hooked from the first chapter, eager to know 'Who done it?' I wasn't disappointed with the conclusion. With various twists and turns, my interest was piqued throughout." —Michele Hall

"Her characters are very real...I love Cinnamon!" —Pam

"Cinnamon Greene dives again. And with luck, she'll continue to until all the dive operators realize dead bodies show up when she's around. *Murder Dives the Caribbean* is the third book in the series. As with the first two, it's a fun to read, fast paced mystery with enough plot twists to keep things interesting....If you like diving, mysteries or both, you'll probably enjoy this book." —Tab